"We never **...** ***ing***
ourselves

"No, we didn ... ... wanted to lie ... him her name. "Yo ...

"Now that I see that hair clearly, oh, yeah," he said. "I'm afraid I know."

Well, if he'd lived on this ranch his whole life, she couldn't be that surprised. The feud was the stuff of Texas legends. Any long-standing family war over good cattle land was enough to make a story last. Throw in priceless jewels and a high-stakes poker game and you got…a good old tall Texas tale.

She nodded, really hoping he wouldn't be too mad. "I'm Paige McCord."

She held out her hand.

He didn't.

"That's great. Just great." He swore, shook his head in disgust or maybe fury and finally said, "I'm Travis Foley."

Dear Reader,

Special thanks to a man named Tom who—despite the fact that no one should ever do this because you can get killed—explains his love of exploring old mines and talks about how to do it. (Please don't ever try this!)

Also, to Lauren in New York with an eBay store called Diamonds By Lauren, who loves colored diamonds, especially canaries. I've admired many beautiful stones and rings on her site. Wouldn't you know it, it finally paid off. (Hours spent browsing the Internet isn't a waste of time to writers. It's about ideas. Really.) Finally, there is a stone that's found only in the area of Texas around Llano. It's commonly known as Llanite and described on one Web site as "a form of granite with some gemmy looking blue quartz inclusions in it."

No, it's not red. But for this story, it is, and my heroine discovered it and named it something else.

Happy reading,

Teresa Hill

THE TEXAN'S DIAMOND BRIDE

TERESA HILL

SPECIAL EDITION®

Published by Silhouette Books

America's Publisher of Contemporary Romance

Special thanks and acknowledgment to Teresa Hill
for her contribution to
THE FOLEYS AND THE McCORDS miniseries.

 SILHOUETTE BOOKS

Recycling programs
for this product may
not exist in your area.

ISBN-13: 978-0-373-65490-1

THE TEXAN'S DIAMOND BRIDE

Copyright © 2009 by Harlequin Books S.A.

Visit Silhouette Books at www.eHarlequin.com

Printed in U.S.A.

TERESA HILL

lives within sight of the mountains in upstate South Carolina with one husband, very understanding and supportive; one daughter, who's taken up drumming (Earplugs really don't work that well. Neither do sound-muffling drum pads. Don't believe anyone who says they do.); and one son, who's studying the completely incomprehensible subject of chemical engineering (Flow rates, Mom. It's all about flow rates.)

In search of company while she writes away her days in her office, she has so far accumulated two beautiful, spoiled dogs and three cats (the black panther/champion hunter, the giant powder puff and the tiny tiger stripe), all of whom take turns being stretched out, belly-up on the floor beside her, begging for attention as she sits at her computer.

With special thanks to my mother, Rachel McIntosh, who accompanied me to Texas by plane and then on a lovely road trip from Dallas through the Texas Hill Country to San Antonio and Austin. We found San Antonio lush, green and beautiful, ate in a café in Austin with a huge rattlesnake skin on display above our booth and discovered that, for some reason, there are no acceleration lanes on Texas highways! (Really. There aren't. Why? Acceleration lanes are a very good thing.)

Chapter One

Paige McCord lay stretched out on a hilltop about a mile away from Travis Foley's Texas ranch, peering through a pair of high-powered binoculars for the third day in a row of her little surveillance mission.

It was early November, the temperatures warm for that time of year but not oppressively so for this sort of outdoor activity, the fall foliage of the Texas Hill Country at its stunning peak.

But Paige hadn't come to check out the sights or enjoy the weather.

Although there was one particular sight she had to admit she was enjoying.

And there he was.

Paige checked her watch. Nearly three-thirty.

"A tad late today, aren't you?" she asked him, adjusting the binoculars to pick up his image as he headed up the dirt trail toward the old mine entrance.

Paige was twenty-six, born and raised in Texas. She was not the kind of girl to have her head turned easily by some cowboy just because he spent his whole life working outdoors, obviously doing very physical work. Which she admitted tended to make a man lean as could be, and yet beautifully muscled, his skin pleasantly browned by the sun.

There was a certain walk cowboys did, an easy, loose-hipped swagger, in jeans that tended to be worn thin over the years, faithfully following every dip and swell of a man's body.

The look was completed by an expensive pair of boots, scuffed up by hard work over the years and a cowboy hat—not one that was for show—and a little late-afternoon stubble on his face, because he would have gotten up before the sun, and the days were long.

This man had all that, but she'd seen all that before.

And she had things to do, she reminded herself, things that were much more important than admiring a good-looking man.

Everything in her life seemed to be changing, changing too much and too quickly, and it had thrown her harder than any horse that had ever managed to unseat her.

Paige's two older brothers had just gotten engaged, and Paige hoped they knew what they were doing, but wasn't so sure. It had all happened so fast.

Tate, her second-oldest brother, had come home from two tours of duty as an Army surgeon in the Middle East and never been the same. She'd been worried about him for a while. Then he'd dumped his fiancée, Katie, whom Paige really liked, and in no time flat, was engaged to the McCord family's longtime housekeeper's daughter, Tanya. Paige liked Tanya. She did. She'd just always thought Tate would end up with Katie, that Katie would take good care of Tate and finally be a McCord.

Then Blake, her oldest brother, had suddenly decided he wanted Katie for himself, and Katie had just agreed to marry him!

Paige still didn't know exactly how all that had happened, she just hoped neither of her brothers had been hurt, and she didn't want them fighting with each other. The family had enough to worry about without her two older brothers feuding.

Her cousin Gabby, who was practically Italian royalty and the spokesperson for the McCord family's jewelry empire, hadn't settled for just an engagement. Gabby had run off with her bodyguard and married him!

It was enough to make Paige's head spin.

Then, there was her twin sister, Penny, who'd been acting weird all summer, always sneaking off somewhere, keeping all sorts of secrets, and normally Paige and Penny never kept secrets from each other. The last time Paige had talked to Gabby, Gabby had asked all sorts of questions about Penny that Paige couldn't answer. Gabby was sure something was wrong.

Not that any of the McCords were acting like themselves lately and not just because of the flurry of romances.

It was their mother.

And their youngest brother.

And their father, dead for five years now.

None of them were what they seemed to be. Her family wasn't at all what Paige had always believed it to be.

She was still so mad—and so shocked—she hardly let herself think about it, but her mother, Eleanor, had confessed this summer to the entire family that she'd long ago been involved with Rex Foley, the patriarch of a family that had been feuding with the McCords since Civil War days.

Not only been involved with him before she'd ever married Paige's father, but had a child with Rex years later! Paige's adorable youngest brother, Charlie, born after Paige's parents had separated briefly when Paige was a little girl, was actually Rex Foley's son!

Paige remembered, barely, a time when their family's Dallas mansion had been filled with tension. She and her sister, Penny, had hidden together in corners all over the house, trying to avoid the angry voices and all the tears their mother cried, their father gone, supposedly just on a long business trip.

In fact, it was the last time Penny remembered the whole family being so tense until this awful summer.

Back then, her father had eventually come home. Her mother finally stopped crying all the time, and then Charlie was born. Adorable, silly, happy Charlie.

Paige and her sister had been five when he was born, and they thought he was the best present they'd ever received, playing with him as if he was one of their dolls come to life.

She'd thought everything was fine then, and it had seemed that way for so long.

But it had all been a lie.

It was still hard to even comprehend how many lies had been told or what would happen to them all from this point on. It was hard for her to even think about it for too long. She had tried to keep busy and then, thankfully, had found a job to do for her family.

A very important job.

She was happy to have a reason to be out of Dallas right now and away from all the tension at the McCord mansion.

Happy to be lying in the grass on a gorgeous November day, staring through her binoculars at a man who was every bit as gorgeous and distracting.

He climbed off of his chestnut-colored horse, let the horse take a nice, long drink from the stream nearby, then—looked like it was going to be Paige's lucky day—started unbuttoning his chambray shirt.

Oh, my.

He pulled a bandana from his back pocket, then he bent over and dipped the bandana in the stream and turned around to face her.

Paige jerked the binoculars away from her face, as if he had a hope of seeing her from this far away. She'd just been so surprised, looking him in the face, even at a distance.

Although to be honest, she couldn't see his face that well from this distance. Still, it looked like he'd winced at something.

She got the binoculars again, found him and saw him cooling off in the stream, washing off some of the grit from working outside all day.

Looked like he'd landed in the dirt at some point.

Not that she objected.

He lifted his face to the sun and let the water from the bandana run down his face, his neck, run in a line down what looked like a perfectly sculpted set of muscles in his chest and rock-hard abs.

Oh, my.

That water had to be cold, she thought. The days tended to be warm right now in the hill country, but the nights were cooler, dipping into the forties the past few nights.

She knew because she was camping out in the national park that lucky for her was just a few miles west of Travis Foley's ranch. Because there certainly wasn't much of a town anywhere nearby, and a stranger staying in a little town like Llano would be noticed.

And Paige couldn't afford to have anyone—particularly Travis Foley—know she was here.

She went back to watching her cowboy, who'd ridden by this particular spot for the last two days in a row, working hard. She thought he was probably doing grunt work, rounding up strays, checking fences and watching for trespassers, while the boss, Travis Foley, likely sat in his air-conditioned mansion somewhere on the edge of the property, counting all his family's oil money or checking on investments or something cushy like that.

She couldn't imagine a Foley working his ranch day-to-day.

He had men like the one she was watching for that.

He finished cleaning up, put the bandana down and buttoned up his shirt. Then he leaned back against that big rock and lifted his face to the sky, like a man admiring the fall sunshine or the still-warm afternoon breeze.

Or maybe like a man worn-out, whether by his work or his own problems, she didn't know.

Or a man who just really needed to get away from it all, to relax here in the peace and quiet of this empty corner of Travis Foley's ranch.

If Paige had time, she might like to enjoy some peace and quiet with him, maybe even a little time in the dark.

It wasn't the kind of thing Paige did, pick up a stranger for the night.

But the summer had been just awful, and sometimes she got to the point where all the problems, all the changes kept racing around in her head, one after another, piling up in there, the pressure building until she just wanted to scream.

This man, this cowboy…surely he could make her forget.

Even if it was just for a night. Not that she had time for that, either. But a woman could dream, couldn't she?

In the meantime, she had work to do.

Once he left, she'd have a full twenty-four hours before he was back again, if the pattern of the last three days held. She had all her equipment with her in her backpack and was a little uneasy about going into the old silver mine alone—anyone who knew anything about old mines would be—but she'd taken every precaution she could.

And she was determined to do this. Her family needed her. She'd promised her brother, Blake, who was CEO of the family's jewelry empire.

Paige stopped thinking about her cowboy. If she did her job right, she'd never even meet him. What a shame.

She put down her binoculars and pulled out her satellite phone. Regular cell coverage was lousy out here in the middle of nowhere.

Blake answered on the second ring, sounding anxious. "Well?" he asked.

"I'm set. I'm going in," she told him. "You know what to do?"

"If I don't hear from you by dawn, I call your friend in the mining department at the university and we come find you," he promised. "Paige, are you sure this is safe? I couldn't stand it if anything happened to you."

"The mine's been there for a hundred years. Travis Foley let a group of archaeologists in there last year to document the petroglyphs on the walls. I got a copy of their report. The place is stable as can be—"

"Still, isn't it dangerous to go in there alone?"

They'd been through this. They'd agreed. No one else could know. Too much was at stake.

Blake merely claimed things were difficult right now financially for the jewelry stores, but that he was handling it. Which is likely what Paige's proud, stubborn, determined oldest brother would say if the world was about to come to an end. He'd be sure he could save it all on his own.

And she was just as determined to help him.

She didn't think the world was coming to an end, just that the problem with the stores was a serious one, and one problem to do with her family that she could actually solve. And she was determined to do just that. Solve it.

"Blake, I'm working on my PhD in geology. I know what I'm doing. Besides, I was in that mine myself weeks ago, just to make sure the reports were right and to make sure I had the equipment I'd need. Trust me. Everything will be fine."

Actually, if her cowboy was the one who caught her, Paige didn't think she'd mind all that much. She was confident she could talk her way out of trouble, if she had to, and she'd be long gone before the news ever got back to Travis Foley that anyone was here.

"I heard the Foleys are having some big family meeting this weekend, which means Travis Foley should be on a plane headed for Dallas by now. So you shouldn't have to worry about him."

"Good." He was one person Paige really didn't want to run into.

"But what about the weather?" Blake asked. "There are some nasty storms predicted from that hurricane in the gulf—"

"Storms that aren't supposed to arrive until tomorrow in the area north of here. I checked the weather radar myself this morning. I'm going in now, and I'll be out before the storm hits tomorrow," Paige told her brother. "You worry too much. I'll be in touch by morning."

Travis Foley got back on his horse and headed up the rise to the rock overhang that hid the entrance to the old mine at the far corner of the 6,500-acre ranch he called home.

It had been his grandfather's before him, his absolute favorite place to be as a child. Out here where he could breathe, where in the quiet he could think and find some peace and do an honest day's work.

The rest of his family, the Foleys, just didn't understand him, and honestly, Travis didn't understand them.

They were oilmen and politicians, big shots out in what they thought was the real world.

This world, to Travis, was real.

It was all the life he wanted, right here.

He wished they'd all just leave him the hell alone and let him enjoy it.

But ever since that old Spanish shipwreck had been found in the Gulf of Mexico, people had gone nuts looking for the Santa Magdalena Diamond, a rock that was supposed to rival the Hope Diamond in size and value.

One of Travis's ancestors, Elwin Foley, had been on that ship when it sank in the 1800s, supposedly along with the diamond and a treasure chest full of old Spanish silver coins.

No one was sure exactly what happened after that. Either the diamond went down with the ship or one of the survivors got away with it. The stone had never been found.

Travis's ancestor survived, bought the ranch on which Travis now lived and started mining for silver. Elwin Foley certainly hadn't lived the life of a man who possessed a fortune in diamonds, working hard on the ranch until he lost his life in a mining accident before ever finding any silver.

His son, Gavin, had even worse luck—raised by his mother alone, barely getting by on the ranch and as a man, developing a gambling problem that led to him losing the ranch and the deed to the old silver mines in the late 1890s in a card game to a man named Harry McCord.

Travis was disgusted just thinking about it and how much the old feud was still alive today between his family and the McCords.

His ancestor, Gavin, had always claimed the poker game was fixed, that Harry McCord was a card cheat. And the McCords had the nerve to strike it rich on the silver mines not long after supposedly winning the deed to the ranch and the mines.

Travis really didn't give a damn. His family had gotten rich in the oil business a few years later. None of them were hurting for money. He didn't begrudge the McCords the fortune they'd built in the jewelry business over the years, a fortune that started with the discovery of silver in the mines.

But he sure begrudged the loss of the ranch.

Because while he lived on the ranch now, as his grandfather had before him, worked it, sweat over it, bled over it, made this place his life, he could never own it.

The McCords did, thanks to a bad hand of poker more than a hundred years ago or a card cheat, depending on which version of the legend a man believed.

Twenty years ago, in an effort to end the bitter feud, Eleanor McCord had offered a long-term lease of the land to the Foleys, which Travis's grandfather had accepted, then come here to make the ranch his own.

Travis had spent the best days of his childhood here and had taken over the ranch when his grandfather died ten years ago. But it wasn't the same as owning the land, and that still had the power to burn a hole in Travis Foley's gut when he let himself think about it too long.

Which was hard not to do when all the hoopla over the stupid diamond and the feud had sprung up again.

Explorers had found the sunken Spanish ship, along with a cache of old Spanish diamonds.

But not the Santa Magdalena.

Which fueled speculation all over again that someone who survived the shipwreck had gotten away with the diamond, and it had long been rumored that person was Elwin Foley, who'd founded the ranch and lived out the rest of his life there.

Which had even more people thinking that the most likely place to find that diamond was right here on Travis's ranch.

Now treasure hunters, gem collectors and even jewel thieves were just showing up here, looking for that cursed diamond. Didn't the damned fools know everyone who'd ever owned it had come to a bad end? Not that it had kept people from looking.

As if Travis didn't have enough to do on a 6,500-acre ranch in November besides keep people from hurting themselves, spooking his cattle, cutting his fences or getting bitten by snakes or something like that.

They'd already kicked five people off the property since the shipwreck was found.

Even worse, Travis's family was convinced the McCords were up to something, something to do with the diamond. Like sending someone to look for it on Travis's ranch.

Had Gavin Foley found it, after he'd supposedly lost the ranch? And hidden it here for one of his ancestors to find later, when one day they might have a hope of owning it free and clear? Finders, keepers?

And had the McCords, after all these years, stumbled upon some clue as to where the diamond might now be?

Travis was highly skeptical of that notion, although his family was not.

He'd finally told them to do what they wanted to figure out what the McCords were up to, that he wanted no part of it. His only concession was agreeing to have someone check each of the mines daily for signs of trouble.

Not just from the McCords but from those damned fool diamond hunters.

Travis had found footprints leading into and away from the Eagle Mine a few weeks ago, had crawled down inside about ten feet and checked things out, but hadn't found anything else.

Still, someone had been there, and it hadn't been him or any of the ranch hands.

So he checked the place himself every afternoon.

Today, everything seemed quiet.

He got off his horse, walked along the long, deep rock overhang, twenty feet wide and at least twenty feet deep, the ceiling sloping downward in the back and at its deepest recess, neatly obscuring the entrance to this particular mine in its dark shadows.

All quiet.

No footprints except his own, which he brushed away with a rake he'd hidden in the brush outside the entrance.

But as he went back outside and stood there, taking a long, cool drink of water from his canteen, he had the oddest feeling.

That someone was out there.

That someone was watching him.

He'd felt the same way at the stream, trying to rinse the dirt off the nasty scratch he'd gotten earlier that day tangling with a barbed wire fence someone had cut.

No one should be out here watching him. From here, it was ranch property for as far as the eye could see, except for that corner of the property that butted up to the national park.

But if someone was watching him, Travis was going to find 'em.

Chapter Two

Paige had to admit, she loved exploring and she didn't get to do as much of it as she liked these days. Too many hours spent at her desk in front of her computer, working on her dissertation.

So she was thrilled in a way to have an excuse to go traipsing through this old mine.

As a highly trained scientist—chief gemologist to her family's worldwide jewelry company, with a master's in geology and hopefully soon a PhD—the idea of discovering a gemstone believed to rival the Hope Diamond was thrilling in a way that had nothing to do with saving the family fortune.

It was the kind of discovery anyone who traveled the world exploring and truly loved the various, extraordinary substances the earth, over time, could yield would have dreamed their entire life about making.

Few scientists ever got to experience the thrill of such a find.

Paige wanted it so bad she could taste it.

Her heart was thrumming so fast it was like a roar in her ears as she stood at the entrance to the mine once her adorable cowboy was gone.

She put down her big backpack, then took out her helmet with her LED light and turned it on, leaving it on the ground to provide some light in the recesses of the overhang that guarded the mine's entrance. From her pack, she pulled out an old pair of coveralls—because exploring was a messy, often cold business. She'd worn her hiking boots in, put one small, spare light around her neck on a cord and another in the smaller pack she'd carry in, along with a small length of rope, spare batteries, power bars and granola, some water, a small notebook and a camera.

Her hair was already in a long braid, which she tucked inside her coveralls. Then she put her helmet on with her LED light wrapped around it. Making sure the light was on, she was ready.

Paige took a breath, let it out slow and off she went into the dark, cool quiet of the old mine.

Travis couldn't believe she went into that mine alone!

He'd hung back, waiting once he'd gotten over the ridge, and there she'd come, a hat tilted low obscuring his view of her face as she hiked over from the ranch's boundary nearest the park.

Looking very efficient, he might add, once he'd crept back close enough and gotten down nearly to ground level so he could watch. She snapped on her light in the deep recesses of the overhang. She suited up, checked her equipment—she'd come prepared, at least—and then seemed to disappear.

He'd been sure there had to be someone else with her, that she wouldn't go inside the mine alone. He'd wanted to catch her companion, too, so he'd waited.

He'd been here when a bunch of archaeologists had explored the mine last year, photographing and documenting the ancient drawings and carvings on the walls called petroglyphs. He had gone inside with them a few times to see what all the fuss was about.

None of the archaeologists had ever gone into that mine alone!

And yet today, there she went!

"Damned, stupid woman!" he growled. His horse gave him an odd look. Travis shook his head. "Not you, Murph," he told the horse.

He climbed into the saddle and headed for the mine, thinking he just might have her arrested for trespassing. Maybe it would make anybody else think twice before trying what she just did.

He needed to put a stop to this nonsense before anyone got hurt.

At the overhang, he tethered Murphy to a small tree and fished in his saddlebags for an oversize flashlight so he'd at least be able to see a bit in front of him, took off his hat, shook his head and swore some more about lost diamonds, family feuds, treasure hunters and women.

He got to the mouth of the mine and headed after her. The entrance was nearly tall enough that he could stand up without hitting his head.

Nearly.

Apparently the miners weren't quite six feet two inches.

If he hunched over a bit, he could stand and walk. The entrance sloped down, but only slightly, nothing too taxing or too dangerous here.

He had the flashlight on but pointed at his feet, not wanting to warn his little trespasser she was about to get caught.

About fifteen feet in, he came to a vertical shaft that went down twenty feet to the next level and another horizontal shaft.

He'd gone this far before, just not alone. The make-shift ladder attached to the mine wall was metal and had been checked and reinforced just last year, had held his weight just fine then.

Travis hoped to hell he caught her somewhere on the horizontal shaft at the twenty-foot level.

He sure didn't want to have to go any farther and allowed himself to mutter some more about stupid legends, ancient curses and women.

He climbed down the shaft, then stood on the horizontal shaft as it opened up both left and right.

Did she know she wasn't alone by now? Had she heard him? She didn't have that much of a head start, and he would hope she was being more careful and moving more slowly than he was, since she hadn't been here before.

At least, he didn't think she'd been here.

Travis stood there, listening, finally hearing a clank and then a muffled curse in the shaft to the left. He hoped she was at least as frustrated as he was and liked the idea that he might scare her half to death, coming upon her this way in an abandoned mine.

If he did, maybe she wouldn't do anything this stupid again.

He crept along, the light out now, going by the feel of the cool, rock wall against his right hand. He caught a glimpse of light, then of what she was studying.

One of the petroglyphs.

An eagle.

He could see it in the light from her helmet, but had only a vague impression of her, sturdy boots, baggy coveralls and a helmet, her nose practically pressed against the rock onto which someone maybe as long as five thousand years ago had carved an eagle.

He was sure she'd come after the diamond.

So why was she studying the drawings?

Travis backed out of the shaft quietly, slowly, wanting to know what she'd do next.

Finally, she started making her way back to the center of the twenty-foot level. From there, it was either explore the passage to the right or descend again.

This time to a hundred feet.

He thought it was downright creepy being that far underground under solid rock.

Surely she wasn't going to do that.

He waited just down the right-hand passageway, peered around the edge of the wall and there she was, checking out the vertical shaft that descended to the next level.

"God almighty!" he muttered, then walked over there and grabbed her around her waist and picked her up as she knelt on the ground peering into a hole, seemingly comfortable as could be, with an eighty-foot drop beneath her.

She screamed so loud he thought she might bring the walls down around them, and he lifted her up in the air and held her there, her body curled up in a ball, mad as hell. She kicked out with her feet and got some leverage against the opposite wall, sent him tumbling back and hitting the wall behind him none too gently.

He held on, one arm around her waist and one managing to get a grip that flattened both arms against her body.

When she finally stopped screaming, he muttered into her ear, "Hush. There's no place to run, and I'm sure as hell not letting you climb down any farther into this mine."

She stopped struggling, finally. She had lost her helmet at some point and its light was now shining down the passageway to the right, so he couldn't see her and she couldn't see him.

He could feel her breathing hard, and didn't feel in the least bit guilty about manhandling her this way, at least not until she calmed down. He wasn't going to let her flounder around and hurt herself or get lost, or God forbid, fall down the eighty-foot vertical shaft in the dark.

"You scared me half to death!" she told him finally, still breathing hard and spitting mad.

Travis eased back just enough to turn her around in his arms, her back against the opposite wall of the mine, then held her there with his own body pressed hard against hers.

"Yeah?" he said, his face so close to hers he could feel the breath coming out of her body. "And you scared me. Do you have any idea how dangerous it is to come into a place like this alone?"

"I know what I'm doing. I'm a grad student in geology at the university," she claimed.

"Do you also know you're trespassing on private property?" he tried, looming over her in the dark, determined to have his say.

"Well...yes," she conceded, finally.

He eased back, still holding her there with his body, but not up in her face, the way he had been.

She was a tiny thing, he'd realized when he'd had her plastered against him just now, slender as could be. Young, too, if she really was a student, like she said.

He didn't think she was going to try to get away any longer, so staying that close to her was more of a distraction than a help at the moment. And he was quickly discovering she had all the necessary attributes to be very distracting to a man.

Travis fought to put those kind of thoughts completely out of his head as he backed away just enough so that he wasn't touching her anymore but could still grab hold of her quickly if he needed to.

"You know if I haul you out of here and call the sheriff, he'd treat you to at least a night in jail," he said.

She sighed. "You don't really want to do that. Do you?"

"If it kept you from trying some damned fool stunt like this again, yeah, I do."

"Look, I'm sorry. I just—"

"Have to find that stupid diamond? Yeah. I've heard it before—"

"Do you have any idea what kind of an opportunity this is?"

"Oh, yeah. Millions of dollars at stake, and you think all you have to do is find it."

"No. Not the money," she claimed. "Finding it. If the Santa Magdalena Diamond is really somewhere on this ranch, it's the find of a lifetime. Scientists spend their whole lives studying and searching, and most of them will never discover anything like this. It's amazing! How could anyone who's serious about a career in science pass up that opportunity?"

Travis frowned, hearing the honest enthusiasm in her voice. Same as with those archaeology students and their supervisors who were on the ranch last summer studying the petroglyphs.

He didn't really understand getting that excited or being so fascinated with those drawings, but he'd seen that kind of enthusiasm and pure joy of discovery before in them.

So she took stupid risks, but that yearning to explore, to discover, he at least understood better than those fools out to make millions by simply getting lucky and stumbling upon a treasure. He believed in hard work much more than luck, so he could understand a bit of what drove her and wasn't quite as annoyed as he was before.

And maybe he even envied her that kind of excitement and yearning. Travis, at thirty, was a man content with his life most days. But every now and then, it felt a little too settled, too predictable.

A little empty.

He didn't remember the last time he was as excited about anything as she was about the chance of discovering the old diamond. A feeling he certainly wasn't going to stand in this old mine and try to analyze.

"Come on," he said, finding her helmet and putting it back on her head, wincing as the light hit him square in the face and quickly turning away. "You're done exploring. We're going up top."

She sighed once again. "Couldn't you just let me look around? I mean, we're already here. What's it going to hurt?"

"The next level is a hundred feet below the surface," he told her.

"I know."

She sounded like the idea thrilled her.

Then he realized something. "You know? What do you mean, you know?"

"From the maps," she said.

"You have maps of this mine?"

"Of course. The people who originally worked the mine kept maps. Not as precise as what we'd make today, but you can find those historical documents if you know where to look. And scientists who've explored the mines over the years kept maps, too. I told you, I'm serious about this. It's not a crazy pipe dream to me. I'm a scientist. And you could help me."

"Why would I want to do that?"

She shrugged. He was close enough that he could feel the movement. "For the money?" she tried. "There's supposed to be a jeweled chest full of old Spanish coins, too. Silver coins. I mean, even a cowboy could appreciate the chance to have that kind of money. This could be the kind of fortune that would let you buy your own ranch someday, if you wanted. And…you wouldn't really even have to help me, if you didn't want to. You could just…not tell anybody I was here? Maybe not tell anyone if I came back and searched some more? I'd pay you, if you wanted, just to…not tell anybody what I was doing."

"You'd go back in here by yourself?" he asked incredulously.

"Yes. And you could stay topside, just to be there in case I did get in trouble. All you'd have to do is call for help. I have friends who'd know what to do to get me out."

Travis swore under his breath. "I think you're nuts to take that kind of risk."

"And I think some people spend their whole lives without ever taking a risk at all, which to me is even worse."

He shook his head. "Well, I think this is a ridiculous conversation to be having while buried under tons of rock. Start climbing."

She hadn't climbed more than two steps on the ladder when a howling, whistling sound swept through the mine.

And then, as the howling died down for a moment, there was a tapping sound, far away and not that loud. Like the beating of a drum. Solid objects hitting other solid objects. And then more howling.

"What the hell is that?" he asked, as they both froze for a moment.

He told himself if it was what he feared—falling rocks—he'd have been hit by something already. Unless it was father down inside the mine or up near the entrance and just hadn't made it to them.

Not yet, anyway.

"Wind," she said.

Okay. Yeah. He felt it, now that he wasn't thinking obsessively of being pelted by rocks. Still, that wasn't all.

"Wind and what else?" he demanded.

"I'm not sure," his gutsy explorer said, not sounding nearly as confident as she had been a moment ago.

He swore, feeling every bit of that distance between him and the surface. "Let's get out of here. Now."

She took off for the top, seeming to know her way in the dark a heck of a lot better than Travis did. He went scrambling after her. When he made it to the horizontal shaft near the surface, she found his hand, grabbed it and pulled him along behind her.

The eerie howling got louder with every step they took and at every moment, Travis still expected to have rocks come hurling down on him, but they never did.

He bashed his head a couple of times on the way out, not able to see that well in the tunnel and moving faster than a man of his size should in a shaft of that size.

Near the entrance, she was sure she smelled rain. But there was no way rain would account for the other sound she heard.

The space around them opened up, but it was still oddly dark, and then Travis realized they'd made it out of the mine, to the long, deep rock overhang that created a covered area sheltered from the elements.

Good thing, too, because outside the sky was nearly black, the world around them a gloomy gray. Out in the open, he saw what looked like miniature, eerily white golf balls bouncing off the ground.

Hail.

It was coming down something fierce, pounding into the ground and then bouncing around until it settled for good. The wind sounded absolutely furious, his horse long gone, no doubt realizing weather was coming long before Travis did and taking off for home.

Travis and the woman backed up against the rock wall as far under the overhang as they could get and still stand up. He was breathing hard, bleeding a bit from the gash he'd just gotten on his head, adrenaline still zinging through his whole body.

Looking at her through the grayish light, he felt a little bit foolish for coming near panic back there, a little bit mad at her for putting them both in that situation and very, very grateful to be out of it and safe.

They weren't buried under tons of rocks.

They weren't dying or already dead.

Just in the middle of a nasty storm. Hail or not, it was just a storm.

He shook his head, trying to clear it, then chuckled, then started laughing.

Maybe because it was the last thing he'd expected to be a part of his day. Descending into an old abandoned silver mine shaft chasing a determined, passionate, half-crazy woman, and then seeing his life flash before his eyes for a moment, only to see a moment later that he wasn't in any danger at all.

He wished he could really see her face. The gloom that had descended was like looking through a thick fog, and she'd clicked off her helmet light, which hadn't shown them anything but rain, and nearly blinded him every time she turned in his direction. He had more of an impression of her than anything else, but he knew she was grinning, too.

A moment later, she was laughing. "It's easy to get spooked down there," she admitted.

"I think I was way past spooked," Travis admitted. "And at the speed you climbed out of that hellhole, I'd say you were, too."

"Well," she shrugged. "Yeah. I guess… I mean, I'm really glad I wasn't down there alone when the storm hit."

"Me, too," he said, thinking, scared or not, it was the most excitement he'd had in his life in months, which was surely a sad commentary on his life right now.

So he couldn't really say he was sorry to have found her sneaking into his mine today, and he wasn't sorry he'd gone in after her, either.

Or even that there was a helluva storm raging around them, lightning crackling loud enough that it seemed like it could split the ground wide open in front of them at any moment.

Storms came big in Texas. He used to love storms on the ranch when he was a kid, so wild and loud, like coming over the top of the biggest hill on a roller coaster and then feeling like he was going to come flying out of his seat at any moment.

Feeling like anything could happen in the next instant, and that no one was really safe.

A man needed to feel like that every now and then, no matter how much he loved the solitude and serenity of his land.

He stared at her, again wishing he could really see her, that he had more than those fleeting moments when he'd watched her climb down the rise and disappear into the mine. Unfortunately, then he'd been concentrating on figuring out what she was up to, not what she looked like. He just remembered noticing a tall, slender body and a dark reddish-brown braid of hair hanging down her back. And he wasn't going to ask her to turn on her helmet light just so he could see her better. They needed to save the batteries, anyway.

She went still, then backed up a bit, and he had to catch her before she went too far.

"You're gonna bump your head if you take another step backward," he said, holding her by the arms, and then putting a hand at the back of her head, between her and the rock overhang. "Right there."

She touched his right temple, her fingers cool and soft against his skin. "You already bumped yours. It's bleeding."

He kept hold of her head and leaned into her touch, too, gentle as could be.

She had on a pair of coveralls that hid every bit of her body. Her dark hair was pulled back from her face and tucked inside the coveralls, her face turned up to his, his body shielding hers from the worst of the wind.

"Do you think it's the hurricane?" she asked.

"I'm not sure."

"Because it's not supposed to be here. It's supposed to stay well north of here—"

"You want to try telling the storm that?" he asked her.

"And it wasn't supposed to get this far inland until tomorrow. I checked."

"Yeah. I did, too. But the weather out here isn't always as predictable as we'd like."

She pouted a bit, and he tried to ignore how cute that little pout looked to him. "I'm just saying...I was careful about everything, and I was watching the weather to make sure it would be okay, and now...well, I guess we're not going anywhere fast in this."

"No, we're not."

He couldn't say he actually regretted that, either.

Chapter Three

Travis tried not to look too eager at the likely prospect of being trapped here all night with her, because he didn't want to scare her, and a woman caught alone for the night with a man she didn't know would have to be a little scared.

So he backed up until the rain blowing in on the wind hit his back in a fine spray, then moved to the side, giving her some space to think things through.

A man who spent his life working the land, often long distances from the ranch house, got caught out in the elements. It was just something that happened. If she'd spent any time in the field as a geologist, she'd probably been caught out in storms, too.

No big deal.

They had shelter from the rain and could likely wait out the storm here just fine, at least until morning light.

He gave up studying her as best as he could through the gloom—it wasn't getting any easier to see—and went with his impressions of her, what he felt she was like. Calm, practical and then…something else.

"You look like you're up to something," he said.

She shrugged. "I'm just thinking that…I'm glad we're out of the rain," she tried.

"Yes." He nodded. "And?"

"And…that…I've been caught in worse weather than this."

"Me, too," he agreed. But that wasn't it, either.

"My Jeep is just over the ridge, maybe a mile away, just across the boundary into the park. I don't suppose—"

Lightning crackled across the sky, then landed with a giant boom.

He could swear he saw her flinch as it hit.

Little Ms. No-Fear was actually afraid of lightning? At least a little bit?

"You really don't want to take a chance on getting hit by lightning," he said.

"I know," she said, like a woman who really knew what a lightning strike could do. "I just thought…the Jeep isn't that far—"

"Even if we didn't have the lightning to contend with, in a downpour like this, the soil out here turns to the consistency of warm mush."

She sighed. "I was afraid of that."

It happened in Texas with its fine, silty soil not accustomed to this kind of rain. It was like trying to walk through quicksand when it suddenly got wet.

"Hey, what happened to your horse?" she asked.

"Long gone. He doesn't like lightning, either, wouldn't leave me for anything but that. Wasn't much around here to tether him to that could actually hold him, if he decided to run, just some scrawny bushes. He would have uprooted the thing by turning his head."

"Oh, okay…. So, for us… What about in the morning? Surely the lightning will have stopped, and we can make it to the Jeep then, can't we?" she said.

"Maybe, although it's still not easy getting any real traction for a while after this kind of storm passes through. Not off-road. You are off-road there, aren't you?"

"By a couple of miles," she admitted.

"Don't worry. If we can't get to your car, there's an old hunting cabin a mile or so from here and high ground between us and it. We'll go at first light, as long as the lightning's through, and hold up there. The ranch hands will be out, checking to make sure everything's okay. Someone from the ranch will find us before long."

"And this spot where we are? It won't flood?"

"Not overnight. If it's still raining like this tomorrow during the day, tomorrow night it might. But don't worry. I've lived on this ranch for the better part of twenty years, know every inch of the place. I know how to keep you safe here, Red, and I'll do it, too."

"Red?"

He grinned. "It is red, isn't it? I can't be sure in this light, but I thought when I watched you walk down to the mine entrance—"

"Yes, my hair is red," she admitted.

"Thought so." He didn't say she had the fiery temperament to go along with it. "So, is this a problem? Spending the night here? Because there really isn't anything else to do—"

"I know. I believe you," she claimed. "So, I guess we should probably…get comfortable. Since we'll be here for the night. Right?"

He nodded. "Are you afraid of me, Red?"

"No." She vehemently denied it.

"Because there's no reason for you to be. I'm not gonna hurt you. Or do anything to you. We're just in this together now, and really, it's a little bit of nothing. One slightly uncomfortable night. That's all. Might as well make the best of it."

He was right. Paige knew he was. No way she could argue the point.

It was just…well, the lightning, for one thing. She hated lightning.

And spending the night with him.

She'd been daydreaming about that very thing when she watched him with his horse by the stream earlier, and she'd felt perfectly safe doing that. Fantasizing about being the kind of woman to just let herself go for a night with a perfect stranger.

She'd never been the kind of woman to let herself do that. A girl growing up with money in a very public way… Well, her father had warned her and her sister early on that there would be boys who wanted her for her money, and she, of course, hadn't listened. It was one lesson she'd learned the hard way, and it had hurt. She'd always been a bit cautious around men since then, a bit distrustful of their motives when they claimed to want her, and she just couldn't be sure they didn't really want a rich woman.

Still, it was a little disconcerting, the way she'd been thinking of him, and to now find herself about to get one night alone with him.

Almost like the world had heard her longing for a man—this man—and delivered him to her.

Paige didn't think the world worked that way.

At least, it never had for her.

She shook her head to clear it of such foolish thoughts, and then started emptying her pockets, taking inventory as she went.

"Let's see what we've got. Extra flashlight, extra batteries for the flashlights, a couple of power bars, some high-energy granola mix, a small bottle of water, a small notebook and a camera. And I hiked in with a backpack, stashed it under the bushes by the…" Her voice trailed off as she saw that he was already headed in that direction. "You were watching me earlier?"

"Yes, I was," he admitted, going right to the spot where she'd left her backpack, finding it with no hesitation at all and bringing it back to her.

She wanted to protest, but how could she? She'd done the same thing, spied on him.

She took the pack from him and started pulling things out. A bigger bottle of water, some more granola, some matches, a survival blanket, which he took and looked over appreciatively.

"That will come in handy tonight."

Then she pulled out her satellite phone.

He shot her a pointed look.

"I'm not stupid. I didn't go in without telling someone what I was doing. If my brother doesn't hear from me by 6:00 a.m., he'll be here soon after that to get me out." She hesitated with the phone, then looked out into the storm. "Do you think—"

"No way," he said. "Not in this."

She tried anyway. "I have to," she told her cowboy. "My brother will go nuts before this storm is over."

Of course, he was right.

No signal.

She put the phone away and hoped she could reach her brother by morning, because he would be frantic otherwise and if the flooding kept him from getting here to her… Well, it would not be pretty.

Her brother thought he could move mountains. And he would to get to her if he thought she was in trouble, and then their whole plan to find the diamond would come out. If the Foleys knew what Paige was up to, she'd have to fight to set foot on this land again.

Yeah, she had to reach Blake by first light, if not sooner.

Paige made herself keep going with her unpacking, until she came to a thick, warm sweater and a fitted pair of sweatpants. She unbuttoned her coveralls and slid out of them, pulling on a second layer of clothes over her jeans and tank top, in favor of the coveralls, which were grimy and dusty from the old mine.

She and Travis shared some granola and water, watched the storm for a bit and then he suggested they might as well bed down for the night. It was early, but the sooner they slept, the sooner they'd wake up and could try to get out of here.

Paige looked over their options. "That spot's the most sheltered, the farthest out of the rain."

He nodded.

She took her coveralls and spread them out on the cold ground right against the back wall of the overhang and motioned for him to make himself comfortable.

As she suspected, he planned to sit up and watch the storm, settling himself with his back to one wall, facing out toward the gloomy night.

"You're sure this area isn't going to flood that quickly?" she asked.

"Reasonably sure, but I'm not taking any chances," he said. "I'm going to watch and make sure."

She sat down beside him, thinking to watch the storm herself.

"There's no reason for both of us to stay up all night," he said. "Or for both of us to be uncomfortable. Come on, Red. I won't bite."

He held out an arm to her and she settled against his side, finding a welcome heat and a body that was hard-muscled, but not as hard as the ground.

He put the survival blanket over her and still had enough left over to cover about half of him, and soon she was toasty warm, her head on his chest, her whole side plastered to his.

She felt his hand at the side of her face, covering her eyes and blocking the lightning, at least a bit.

"Go to sleep," he said. "I won't let anything hurt you."

She tried. Really tried.

But the wind slowly and steadily picked up, the fierceness of the storm growing with every moment. Every bolt of lightning had her struggling more and more to cover her fears, to stay still, to keep breathing easily and deeply, when all she wanted to do was get as close to him as possible and beg him to make it all stop.

It was a foolish thing, being afraid of something as simple as a storm, and yet, there it was. Caught in this eerily dark world, she was afraid.

And there was so little in life she truly feared.

She worked her face deeper into the curve between his shoulder and his neck and closed her eyes. "It is the hurricane, isn't it? The way the winds keep building. It's… That's what hurricane winds do."

"Yeah, it looks like we got the hurricane," he told her, arms holding her tight.

"So we just sit here and see how much worse it gets?" That seemed completely unreasonable.

"Not much else to do, Red."

"I mean, we don't know how much worse it's going to get or when its going to stop—"

"No, we don't."

"Tornadoes spring up from these storms when they're over land—"

"Sometimes," he admitted.

"Tornadoes, lightning, flooding. Perfect night—"

She broke off with a gasp as a huge clap of thunder drowned out her words.

He scooped her up and deposited her sideways on his lap, even closer than she had been to him, draped the blanket around her and grinned as he looked down into her eyes.

"You know, I could make you forget," he said.

"What?"

"The storm. That you're afraid—"

She sputtered, surprised and furious. "I am not afraid!"

"Red, you flinch every time a bolt of lightning strikes. Not a lot, and I know you're fighting it, but you do. And that's fine. I mean, it's no big deal. We're all afraid of something, and I'm just saying, I'm here. I'm happy to be of help, to get you through the night. Whatever it takes."

Paige shook her head, having a hard time thinking, between being on guard about when and where the next bit of lightning might strike and trying to hide her fears and then having this man…this altogether tempting specimen of man make her an offer of…what, exactly?

"Are you saying, you'll…that you'll—"

"Whatever you want," he said smoothly, a hint of amusement and, she thought, sheer wickedness in his tone.

"You think I would be so caught up in you and whatever you were doing to me, that I'd forget all about the storm and being afraid? You think you're that good?"

"I'm saying I'm willing to try, that I'd certainly give it my best shot. I mean…I managed to distract you for the last few moments, didn't I?"

"I—I—I can't believe you—"

"You haven't flinched over the last two lightning strikes, in case you didn't notice. So from where I sit, it seems to be working."

From where he sat!

Well, from where she sat, she was… She was on top of him, all lean muscles and heat and…and…

She had pushed herself upright at one point, wasn't snuggled against him as she had been at first, but she was still sitting on his lap, her hands pressed against his chest for balance and to keep her from getting any closer.

"I don't… I just…I don't do this."

"Do what? Snuggle? Kiss? Play around a little?"

Play around a little?

"That's what you're offering to do?" she asked.

He shrugged easily. "I'm saying I'm open to the possibilities."

He made it sound so innocent, like nothing of consequence at all. Like passing the time in casual conversation or something.

"Actually," he said. "Now that I think about it, not absolutely anything. We couldn't actually have sex. No condoms. I don't generally ride around the ranch prepared in that particular way."

"Not an opportunity that normally presents itself during a normal workday at the ranch?" she quipped.

"No, Red. I have to say, it just doesn't happen. Damned shame, don't you think? I love working this ranch. Something like that happened every now and then… Well, I'd have to say the job would be just about perfect then."

"Get lonely out here, Cowboy?"

He nodded.

She shook her head. "I can't decide what to make of you. If you were half-serious about that or just…just—"

"I was going to kiss you," he admitted, laughing

beautifully, that rich, deep voice of his wrapping around her like a spell in the dark. "Although I am up for just about anything you'd like. I mean…a man needs to take care of a woman. It's just…what a man does."

"Make the sacrifice? Since I'm afraid and everything?"

"Yes, ma'am."

"Is this some cowboy code you live by? You're honor bound to offer your body to a woman in distress—"

"That's just what a man does."

Paige didn't know whether to be embarrassed or charmed.

Both, probably.

"I don't know what to say," she admitted.

"You don't have to say anything. I was just letting you know you had options."

"Oh, well. Options. Okay."

"But really, why don't you just stay here with me, lean down against me." He eased her down against his chest. "There you go. And let your head go right here." Against that warm, inviting curve of his shoulder and his neck. "That's it. Close your eyes."

He spread the blanket over her and him. She could feel him breathing deeply and easily, feel the heat of his body, his heartbeat beneath one of her palms.

He put one of his hands over her ear, and with the other ear buried against his chest, it blocked out a lot of the sound, making a little cocoon of safety for her.

It was nice.

Really nice.

"Go to sleep," he whispered. "You'll be fine."

* * *

She tried.

She really did.

But the storm kept going. She'd be nearly asleep, then find herself jerked out of that half sleep by lightning, feel his arms tighten around her to let her know she wasn't alone, feel the glorious heat of his big, hard body, and then find herself thinking of what he'd offered.

It was just a night.

Just a little comfort in the dark on a big, scary night.

She knew lightning wasn't going to come snaking inside the rock overhang and get her. It wasn't chasing after her.

But an irrational fear was just that—an irrational fear.

And she'd been battling this one since she was a little girl and had gotten caught in her tree house during a big storm. No one had known she was there, and she'd stayed well hidden inside of it, huddled into a little ball, shaking and crying like she never had in her life. Her mother's face had gone absolutely white when she realized her daughter had been in a tree during a lightning storm. To Paige, it had seemed like it had gone on forever, like no one would ever come and save her, that the lightning would surely reach out and get her at any moment.

"I was playing outside when I was five or six, and a storm came, and I took shelter at the closest spot, which turned out to be my tree house," she finally admitted.

"Oooh," her cowboy sympathized.

"Yeah, not the best place to be during a storm. It was awful, and it seemed like forever before anyone found me."

He held her tight as she lay draped over him, bracing for the next boom of thunder. His hands moved gently over her shoulders, trying to soothe and work out some of the tension there. She snuggled closer, her face pressed as far into the curve of his neck as she could get it, the reassuring rise and fall of his chest beneath her, the beat of his heart, steady as could be, thumping against one of her ears.

"I could tell you a story," he whispered.

And she grinned despite her fears. "Thank you, but I'm not five years old anymore. Besides, I never got bedtime stories. I got songs. My mother used to sing us to sleep."

"Okay, I'm definitely not singing. You don't want me to sing."

"Then...I guess there's not much else you could do," she said, thinking it came out sounding like an invitation more than anything else.

Oops.

She didn't mean it that way.

Honestly, she didn't.

So what if he was here? She was here. The storm was here. And it was going to be a long night.

He took her face in his hand, eased back away from her, just enough that he could look her in the eye and said, "Let's just try one kiss, Red. Okay? One. And we'll see how it goes from there."

Well, if he thought she was going to fight him off....

No, he knew she wasn't going to do that.

Just let go, she told herself. *It's just one night, just one kiss.*

He let his mouth settle over hers, firm and sure, insistent and yet moving like a man who had all the time in the world. She opened herself up to the kiss, to him. To the heat and the pleasure, falling into it.

Some men just knew how to touch a woman, when to linger, when to blaze forward, when to tease and when to take.

He knew.

He devoured her, and she let him, helped him as best she could, with long, hungry kisses and hands that roamed restlessly across his chest, his shoulders, his back, into his hair, trying to get even closer.

She wasn't altogether sure how she got there, but she ended up straddling his lap, her hips in his hands, her breasts crushed against his chest, wishing she didn't have a stitch on.

And it all happened as fast as a fire roaring out of control.

"Damn, Red," he said, lifting his mouth from hers long enough to catch a ragged breath.

"I know."

Maybe she'd just been alone too long, gotten too caught up with her work and her family and all of its craziness. Had forgotten to make time for Paige, the woman, with all a woman's needs.

Because this felt very much like need.

He kissed her again, used his hands on her hips to draw her into a rhythm against him that was both arousing and maddening through their clothes.

If he'd laid her down on the hard ground right then and started stripping her clothes off, she didn't think she could have stopped him. She was so aroused already he might not even have to take her clothes off her. If he just kept doing what he was doing, which now included a hand slipping beneath her sweater and her shirt and that little nothing camisole of a bra to her breast, his mouth on her neck…

Her whole body gave a shudder.

The things he was doing to her neck….

He laid her back against that hard ground, settled himself heavily, but still fully clothed, on top of her, pushed up her clothes and took her nipple into his mouth and sucked hard.

"Trust me, Red," he muttered. "Just trust me. Everything will be fine."

Chapter Four

Paige slept like a baby.

Blissfully, heavily, completely unaware of anything, until she woke to the same sound of pounding rain and howling wind of the night before. If anything, it might just be worse.

And she was alone.

She sat up, wiped her hair from her face. It was flying around everywhere this morning, escaping from her braid. Her shirt and her camisole were bunched up under her sweater, and she straightened those, her cheeks filling with heat at just how that had all happened. And her jeans were unbuttoned, unzipped.

And she couldn't say she was sorry at all.

They hadn't actually had sex.

Not quite.

But he certainly had taken care of her.

She'd felt like the whole world exploded quite happily inside of her, with nothing but his mouth and his hands, and felt bad that he hadn't let her do the same for him.

But he'd said he wanted her in a nice, soft, warm bed, in a nice, warm bedroom with all the time in the world to do this right. He didn't want to be rushed. He didn't want to be worried about the storm or a flood, and he kind of liked the idea of her owing him.

So there it was.

She owed him.

And planned on happily making good.

Lord, what a man!

Then she remembered the money thing. Paige's family had serious money. And clout. And history.

Men could get weird about it.

She hoped her cute cowboy didn't get too weird about it. Ranch hands lived simply, most of them on very little, and usually had a healthy disdain for the world in which Paige's family lived.

She just wanted to know the man, enjoy the man, think for a while at least that any and all good things were possible with the man.

How long had it been since she'd felt like that?

She was practically singing as she got to her feet and went to look for him.

It was still very early, not quite five her watch told her, the world still filled with a ghostly white gloom, the rain not retreating in the least. Neither was the wind.

She went from one end of the overhang to the other. It was like searching through thick fog, but he wasn't there.

A moment later he came in out of the rain, a ghostly

image, except she could tell he was dripping wet. He stopped when he spotted her and then through the gloom, she could swear she saw his mouth spread into a big smile.

"Sleep well, Red?"

"Yes, I did," she said. "You?"

"I had really nice dreams and a woman draped all over me. Yeah, I slept just fine."

So that's how she'd slept? Draped all over him?

It must be true, because she'd slept on rock-hard ground before, and the body made its protests known the next day. Hers felt just fine this morning.

"Sorry about that," she said.

"I'm not complaining," he reassured her.

"No, just... You got to sleep on the ground. I definitely got the better end of the deal."

"Well, you can owe me for that, too, Red."

And then she laughed like she hadn't in years.

Yeah, she owed him.

And it felt good to owe him, to think of paying back the favors of last night, leisurely, happily, in a nice warm bed.

"So, where is this nice, warm bed of yours, and how are we going to get to it?"

"My bed is about five miles, as the crow flies. So we're going to have to make do with the hunting cabin I was telling you about. All we have to do is make it through the rain. I'm glad you've got your boots on. And your coveralls are waterproof?"

She nodded.

"Good. You'll be just fine."

"And you'll be soaked," she said, looking at the shirt

plastered to him, his dark hair drenched and slicked back, lying against his head.

"I've been wet before. I'll survive, and we'll get a nice fire going once we get to the cabin and we can dry each other off. Sound like a plan?"

"Yes, it does," she agreed.

A glorious plan.

They gathered up their things. She had her small pack, and he took her larger one. She got into her coveralls and then stared out into the storm.

At least the lightning had stopped.

Still, what a mess.

"The wind's not any worse than it was last night," she said. "Like…the storm's stalled?"

"Right on top of us, I'd say."

Which was not good.

A fast-moving hurricane could drop a lot of rain quickly, but at least it was gone fast, carried along by the forward movement of the storm.

But sometimes a hurricane came ashore and then ran into another front coming the other way, and it was like a standoff in the sky. The two storm systems just sat there, dumping torrential rain carried by the leftovers of the hurricane on the same spot.

The flooding could be devastating, particularly in a place as flat and normally dry as Texas.

"If I thought this was going to get any easier, I'd say we wait it out. But I really don't think this storm is moving, Red. We need to just trudge through it. We'll stick to the side of the ridge, so we'll have high ground. And it probably won't look like a path, but trust me, it's there and I know it. I grew up on this ranch. Cabin's maybe a mile and a half from here. Stick close to me, and if you need help, yell. Okay?"

"Okay," she nodded, trusting him implicitly.

They set off in the cold, soaking rain, so heavy she could barely see him in front of her. He was right about the path. She didn't see one, but he seemed to know exactly where he was going.

At times, off to the left, she could see what she thought was a raging river, where a peaceful stream had been the day before.

The one she'd watched him wash off in, when she'd had all those wonderful fantasies about him.

He lived up to them and more, she decided, and as soon as they got in out of the rain, she was going to peel those wet clothes off of him, dry him off and then heat him up.

It could rain for a week, for all she cared.

They trudged on through the storm. The ground was wet and had the consistency of watery oatmeal under her feet. Even with her work boots, she was sliding all over the place.

Rain dripped off her cowboy hat, blew in at times and rolled down her face, her neck and inside the opening of her coveralls, no matter how tightly she clutched them to her. It soaked through her sweater, her shirt, even her socks.

Yuck!

The sky lightened only marginally as they walked and, presumably, the sun came up somewhere above all the clouds and the rain.

She didn't want to think of what might have happened if he hadn't caught her in the mine. If she'd been inside the mine shaft alone when the storm hit, not knowing for sure what was going on, it would have been a long journey out of there alone. And an even longer night, either huddled alone against the rocks, scared half to death of the lightning or she might have even headed for the Jeep, might not have found it in the gloom, and then what would have happened to her?

Anything.

They trudged on, miserable, cold, wet.

She wondered if the cabin might have a primitive shower or even an old washtub. A bath was highly unlikely, she knew, but a woman could dream, couldn't she?

A bath and then a nice warm bed with him.

That was a fantasy!

In the end, it took more than three hours. Three thoroughly miserable hours, but they made it. Paige didn't see how he found his way, because the world seemed like a wet, foggy, miserable mess to her, but he led them right to a small cabin.

"Come on," he said, opening the door for her.

She wanted nothing more than to get inside, but dug in her pack for her satellite phone instead. It was nearly six, and her brother had to be going crazy.

She huddled under the narrow overhang of the roof, pressed up against the side of the cabin and held up the phone. "I have to try to make a call before my brother shows up with the National Guard or something like that."

He nodded. "I'll start a fire. If you get through, I need to call the ranch, let 'em know I'm okay and to get us when they can."

"Fire!" That was what she heard. "Yes, please. A fire."

He went inside, and she turned on the phone and dialed. There was a ton of static on the line, a couple of seconds when she thought she heard Blake, frantic and calling her name, and then nothing.

Finally, on the fourth try, she could hear him.

"Hey, sorry about that. I got caught in the storm, but I'm fine," she yelled into the phone.

"What?"

"I'm fine!"

"Paige—"

"Out of the mine, taking shelter in a cabin. I'm fine."

"Cabin?"

"Yes. I'm in a cabin. We'll wait out the storm here. I'll call as soon as I can. Don't worry. And don't do anything stupid, like send someone to get me. You'll give our whole plan away. Blake? Blake—"

But he was gone. There was nothing but static now.

Oh, well. *He got the important parts,* she thought. She was safe, out of the mine, out of the storm, and he didn't need to do anything.

Which would be incredibly hard for her big brother, but Paige had to hope that he'd sit tight.

She clicked off the phone and opened the door to the cabin to find no real light, just what she had from her own helmet lamp. Slowly panning the room, she saw a roughly made wooden bed in one corner, a giant fireplace, two chairs, shelves with dry stores of food, a sink and what she really, really hoped was a bathroom behind a door in a corner.

She was still standing on the threshold, literally

dripping wet, when the door opened and out came her cowboy, already out of his wet clothes and into a pair of dry jeans, pulling on a dry flannel shirt.

"I'm afraid there's no electricity, and I was making too much of a mess to do the fire first," he said. "Stay where you are. I'll bring dry clothes to you. Believe me, it's going to be easier this way."

She didn't argue, feeling like a drowned rat and looking away, not wanting anyone, especially him, to see her looking this bad and grateful that there wasn't much light in the cabin yet.

He came back a moment later with a pair of sweatpants and another flannel shirt, even a pair of men's boxers.

"Best I have to offer," he said. "Now, my advice to you would be to get naked right here at the door and drop your clothes where they are. Because there's only one dry towel left, and I imagine you'd rather have it for yourself and not bring all the water and mud into the cabin."

"Did you strip at the door?" she asked.

"No, I just wish I had."

Paige laughed and motioned for him to turn around so she could start stripping. She'd do anything right then to be warm and dry.

He turned to the side and held up the towel between them. She didn't think she'd ever taken her clothes off that quickly. Not that it was easy, since everything was heavy with water and her fingers were practically numb.

But she got them off, leaving them in a sopping pile on the floor in the doorway, then took the towel and wrapped it around herself.

He just grinned and handed her the dry clothes.

"Is that a real bathroom over there?" she asked.

"There's no hot water, if that's what you're asking. But there is running water. Rainwater collection system on the roof, so there's no shortage of water now. Some semblance of a shower, if you could stand the cold. But there is a toilet that flushes and everything."

"That's it. I'm in love with this place," she said, heading across the room for the bathroom. "If there were dry socks somewhere, I'd be in heaven."

"I'll see what I can do," he promised.

"And a fire? Dry socks and a fire? You are my hero!"

"Simple girl, are you? Easy to please?"

"Today I am," she promised, shutting herself into the tiny bathroom.

He'd found a candle in the bathroom and left it burning. The room was tiny, primitive, but clean. She rubbed herself down briskly, dismissed completely the idea of a cold shower right now. Maybe once he got a big fire going, she'd try it. For the moment, she hurried into the boxers, the sweatpants and the flannel shirt.

They felt fabulous. Better than any designer gown she'd ever tried on.

Then she went to work trying to squeeze what water she could out of her hair.

Finally, she wrapped it in the towel and went into the main room.

He had a fire just starting to burn in the giant stone fireplace and she knew they'd soon be warm, given how small the cabin was, once the fire really got going.

She sat down on the raised stone hearth, and her hero presented her with luxuriously thick, warm socks.

"Ahhh!" She moaned in pure ecstasy, then exclaimed, "That's it. It's official. I would do absolutely anything for you!"

"Red, I haven't even made you a cup of hot coffee yet, but I'm about to. What is that gonna get me?"

"I don't know. What do you want?"

"Well, if that fire was going and this place was even halfway warm, I'd have dried you off myself and not given you any clothes to wear. I'd have taken you straight to bed. But I was planning on being gentlemanly about it and warming the place up first, maybe getting some food in you, and then getting you naked. That was my plan."

"That sounds like an absolutely glorious plan."

Okay, just like that.

They had a plan.

A highly satisfying plan.

Travis figured there was only one other thing he absolutely had to do before hauling her off to bed, and that was to try to get hold of someone at the ranch house, just so they'd know he was okay and not waste time trying to find him.

He was sure they had better things to do right now, to make sure everything else on the ranch was okay. He could wait. He might be very happy waiting here with her, letting someone else take care of things for a change.

After all, how many times did he find himself stranded with a gorgeous, willing woman?

It was definitely a first for him. Years of good clean living and hard work were being rewarded right here, he decided. He deserved it and he intended to enjoy it. She would, too. He'd make sure of it.

But first, he took her satellite phone and dialed the ranch. Nothing but static greeted him, despite repeated attempts.

"Try it outside," she suggested, warming herself by the fire, just starting to catch well and throw off some heat and light. "There's just enough of an overhang on the roof to keep you dry, and point the antenna toward the mine. That's where I finally found a signal."

"Okay. Be right back, Red."

He got outside. Lord, it was a miserable day out there, but he was smiling, whistling, even.

He did as she suggested and pointed the antenna toward the mine, and sure enough, there was something of a signal. His housekeeper, a fierce-looking, no-nonsense woman named Marta, answered.

At least, he thought it was her.

The line crackled with static.

"Marta, it's Travis. I'm holed up in the hunting cabin near the Eagle Mine. I'm fine. Tell the men to see to the animals and not to worry about coming to get me until they can."

She said something. He thought she got it. Then asked, "Everything okay there, Marta? Look, tell Jack that the creek near the mine is a roaring river right now, not to be in a hurry to try to cross it to get to me. I'm fine."

He hoped she got that, because the static only got worse. He clicked off the phone and let it be.

He realized he hadn't said anything about his pretty trespasser, but then, what was the point? Nobody there really needed to know, he reasoned.

It was his ranch, and he'd decide for himself what to do with her once they were out of here.

Travis sighed and looked out into the mess of the storm.

He intended to enjoy himself in what time they had here. They'd figure out the rest later.

She sat on the hearth and used the towel to dry her hair as best she could, then finger-combed it to get out the tangles and separate the strands in hopes it might dry faster.

The fire was soon roaring. With that and the light from the half-dozen candles that she found scattered around the room, she could finally see, after hours in the dark and the ghostly gloom. When she had a mug of hot coffee in her hand, her life was nearly complete.

Paige was so busy thinking about what was to come between them that it was only after he'd gone outside and then come back in that she remembered something she should have already discussed with him.

He really had her completely distracted, thinking only of how much she wanted to be curled up in that bed with him naked in his arms.

She looked up as he came back into the cabin, her thoughts warring between him and what she wanted from him, versus her own family and what she'd come here to do.

And she hated asking this of him, bringing this into it, but she had to. She looked up at him and said, "You didn't tell anyone at the ranch what I was doing, did you?"

"No," he said.

But he'd gone still by the doorway, staring at her.

When he stepped closer, into the fall of light from the roaring fire and the candles, she could finally really see him. Not like that glimpse she had through the binoculars when she'd quickly, guiltily looked away. No rain falling between them now, no fog, no storm and no darkness.

He was tall, his body lean and beautifully muscled, hair dark, eyes dark and unfathomable at the moment.

She felt a hint of uneasiness first, a sense that she was missing something, something important that was right in front of her.

"What is it?" she asked, thinking there was something familiar about him. "What's wrong?"

He came close, taking a long strand of her hair in his hand and holding it out in front of the fire.

"It looked so much darker before. But in this light, it's almost like gold," he said. "A golden red."

"Yes." Again, she felt uneasy, and again, she wasn't sure why.

Did he know who she was?

Was that why he was suddenly so wary? Maybe even angry?

Paige's family was Texas's version of royalty, wealthy and often in the spotlight. She and her sister had been in the society pages of the *Dallas Morning News* and all the bigger papers in the state since birth.

And the hair was often what gave her and her sister away.

Not many women had this combination of reddish-gold hair.

"We never got around to introducing ourselves last night, Red," he said.

"No, we didn't." She hadn't wanted to. Hadn't wanted to lie to him and hadn't wanted to tell him her name, just in case it meant something to him. And she'd been happy to think of him simply as her cowboy, a man she'd admired and met by chance. Nothing else. Finally, she found the courage to ask, "You know who I am?"

"Now that I see that hair clearly, oh, yeah," he said. "I'm afraid I know."

Well, if he'd lived on this ranch his whole life, she couldn't be that surprised. The feud was the stuff of Texas legends. Any long-standing family war over good cattle land was enough to make a story last. Throw in priceless jewels and a high-stakes poker game and you got…a good old tall Texas tale.

"One of the twins is a jewelry designer. I'm guessing she wouldn't hold up as well down in a mine. So you must be the scientist," he concluded.

She nodded, really hoping he wouldn't be too mad. "I'm Paige McCord."

She held out her hand.

He didn't.

"That's great. Just great." He swore, shook his head in disgust or maybe fury and finally said, "I'm Travis Foley."

Chapter Five

She laughed despite herself, and said, "No, you're not!"

He nodded, looking like a man not in the mood to be patient with her while she worked this out in her own head.

"You...you were riding around like some ranch hand, checking the fences, checking the livestock. I saw you."

"You were watching me?" he asked incredulously.

"Of course I was. Did you think I'd just show up one day and head down into the mine? With no idea of whether anyone ever came that way? Whether I'd get caught? I watched you for the last three days. Doing the work of a regular ranch hand."

"I'm a rancher. It's what I do. I work the land." He looked furious.

"You're supposed to be in Dallas at some big family meeting," she remembered.

"I didn't feel like going to Dallas for another family meeting," he said bitingly. "And you? You're spying on me? And my ranch?"

"It's not your ranch," she reminded him.

And, *oh, wow.*

That was clearly the wrong thing to say.

He looked like he might strangle her right there where she sat. He was breathing hard, towering over her, looking like he might grab her by her hair and throw her out right then and there.

But he didn't.

He just glowered at her.

"No, it's not my ranch. Believe me, your family would never let mine forget that. You probably wouldn't understand this, but the thing is, a man works a piece of land every day, sweats over it, bleeds over it, takes care of it like it was his, he starts to get ideas he shouldn't have—"

"That's not what I meant," she claimed. "I mean...I know you must...care about the place—"

"Care about it?" He laughed, still furious. "I care about what I have for dinner some nights, whether the Cowboys win a football game, whether it's going to rain or be sunny. What I feel for this ranch is a helluva lot more than care."

"Yes. Okay." She got to her feet, tired of him towering over her, though in truth, he still did even when she was standing. "I'm sorry—"

"So for you to just waltz in here like your family owns the place, which I suppose you think you do, and head down into that mine, like you think you own that, too, to try to find that stupid diamond—"

"Yes. You're right. I'm sorry—"

"To give me that I'm-just-a-grad-student routine? That it's-the-chance-of-a-lifetime routine?" He took her chin in his hand, getting right up in her face and holding her there, glaring at her. "You lie really well, Red."

She shoved him away hard, and then nearly tripped over the stone hearth of the fireplace as she backed away from him.

He swore, reached out to grab her to keep her from falling.

"You really didn't know it was me?" he demanded, his grip on her nearly tight enough to hurt.

"No. Of course not. I told you. I thought you were just a ranch hand. I thought—"

"What?" he demanded.

"Nothing—" She was blushing, just thinking of what she thought. That he was a beautiful man. A beautiful, ordinary man. And of what she'd wanted from him, what she'd let him do.

Oh, Lord, what she'd let him do…

What she'd planned for them to do once they got here…

She swallowed hard, thinking for a moment of all she'd lost in this instant. Glad it hadn't gone any further between them, and yet…

She couldn't believe he was one of the Foleys.

Paige had been introduced to him, of course. A girl didn't move in the upper echelon of Texas society for her whole life without being introduced to the Foleys, even if her family had been feuding with them since the Civil War.

So they'd no doubt exchanged icily polite, icily brief

handshakes at various social functions over the years, charity balls, the governor's mansion, that sort of thing.

There were three brothers, something of a mixed set, all young, wealthy, arrogant and good-looking. In her mind, she could see them standing in a row in black tuxedoes and starched white shirts, looking for all the world like they owned everything they surveyed.

She'd never really been that interested in the feud, in perpetuating it or ending it, had just grown up on tales of how terribly his family had treated hers and been happy to keep her distance from him and the entire clan.

So she'd shook his hand a time or two when forced to do so in the name of good manners and not having any interest in causing a scene.

She really hadn't paid that much attention to the whole brood until her mother's terrible secret had come out this summer.

That her mother had once loved his father, Rex Foley. Her curiosity had driven her to the Internet and the photos she could find. She'd skipped right over the brothers and zeroed in on the father instead.

His father had slept with her mother and fathered a child with her. Paige's little brother, Charlie.

How could that be?

She still couldn't quite believe it, couldn't make sense of it, couldn't...

And all that time she'd been glaring at pictures of Rex Foley, trying to understand, trying to see something of her little brother in him and wondering how it was that they'd managed to keep that secret all these years, how no one had known...

All that time, she should have been looking at the Foley brothers, arming herself, protecting herself against what was to come.

Then she might have known, she might have recognized him from the first. It was just that every time in the past when she'd met him he'd been in a tuxedo, all polished manners and cool, sophisticated charm, dismissive as could be of anyone in her family and disapproving, as well. And while that arrogance might work for some women, Paige had grown up with men like that.

It was old hat to her, a nice-looking man in a tuxedo who acted like he owned the world.

Men like that really didn't do a thing for her.

They just didn't seem real.

That man working the ranch, checking the mine, catching her there... He'd seemed interesting and very real.

So different from any version of Travis Foley she'd ever seen.

Sweaty, a little dirty, in worn jeans and well-worn boots.

A working man.

Real.

Right now he was also furious.

"What?" she asked, lost in her thoughts.

"Before, you said you thought I was a ranch hand, that I was... What? What were you going to say?"

That it would be nice to have someone who looked like you walk right into my life. That I was lonely. That I hadn't had anyone special in my life for a long time and... And...

Oh, God. What did it matter now?

It could never be.

He was Travis Foley.

"I thought you looked like a nice guy," she told him, laughing with as much disgust as she could muster. "How ridiculous is that?"

That seemed to satisfy him for the moment. They retreated to opposite corners of the small room, him leaving her by the fire to get warm while he brooded in the corner by the bed.

A single bed, maybe a single and a half, if there was such a thing.

Paige looked away. She had to forget what happened between them the night before, just completely erase it from her mind. It didn't mean anything, and really, it was nothing. A little flirtation, a little…more than flirting.

Cuddling, kissing, his big, warm body rocking erotically against hers, and all those promises of so much more to come.

Her face burned at the memory.

And then she had a terrible thought.

She got up and glared at him. "You really didn't know?"

"Know what?" he said, his tone biting.

"That it was me? That I was a McCord?"

"No."

She wasn't sure she believed him, although when she thought about it, she honestly wasn't sure how it would have benefited him to lie about it, to pretend. To flirt with her the way he had, and to get her pants off of her and yet still not take it all the way.

Why be a nice guy at that point? If he was looking to just…mess with her head or her body or…

No, it didn't make any sense.

"Red, if I'd wanted you last night, I could have had you a half a dozen times by now, and you know it. So don't go playing the outraged, violated woman with me. It won't fly."

Okay. He could have. And they both knew it.

"Then, I don't understand," she said.

"Understand what?"

Who he was?

Who that man last night had been?

He stared at her from across the room, still angry, but looking more than a little confused now, uneasy, suspicious and maybe even a little vulnerable.

"Nothing. Forget it. I… It doesn't matter now," she said.

He was a Foley. His father had been involved with her mother years ago, fathered a child with her and then walked away. What kind of man was he? What kind of man was the son?

She'd gotten her heart and her ego bruised more than once, and then she'd developed a healthy distrust for men in general, which she'd totally ignored with this man.

What a time to let down that sense of caution.

From outside, the wind came up in a gust that sounded more like a roar. The cabin walls literally shook from the force of it, and the rain kept pounding down.

They ignored each other as best they could for most of the day. He built the fire up until it was roaring. She emptied a few cans of beef stew into a heavy metal pot that hung from a hook over the fire and cooked until it smelled heavenly.

Something about cooking over an open fire and being hungry made it even taste that good.

He was coldly polite, thanking her for the meal, making sure she knew how to hang the pot over the fire and get it off without burning herself, and then keeping to himself on the side of the room farthest from the fire.

Every now and then he went outside, pacing along the side of the cabin under the tiny overhang and staring at the storm.

By nightfall, she'd cleaned the whole place, for lack of anything better to do, fixed another meal of canned ravioli and finished one of only three books she'd found in nooks and crannies in the cabin. A paperback mystery about a wealthy woman whose husband stole every dime she had and ran off, very nearly never to be found again.

It was perfect for her mood right now, when she was thinking you really could never trust a man.

And then she decided she might as well get ready for bed, something she'd been dreading, because there was only one.

She hesitated, not sure what he intended.

From behind her, she heard him say, "Go ahead. Take the bed. I'll sleep by the fire."

"On the floor?"

"We slept on the ground last night, Red, and did just fine."

Yes, they had. Still, she didn't want him to be nice or gentlemanly or anything like that. "You'll get cold," she said.

"Won't be the first time, won't be the last. And tonight we've got a fire."

She nodded, not turning around, not wanting to look at him or to think of what she'd expected this night to be. It was ridiculous, anyway. To think she'd waltz onto the ranch and find this man who did nothing but work the land, an ordinary, hardworking man who wouldn't know about her family's money and power and even if he did, wouldn't care.

Just a man who would get all tangled up in her, practically on sight.

And it was absolutely the last thing she needed to be thinking about right now, with her family absolutely going crazy and their jewelry store empire in some serious financial difficulties, her trapped here with the enemy, caught red-handed trying to steal a priceless diamond right out from under his nose.

Oh, her family would claim ownership if she found it, but it would be a legal fight that could last years, and she'd be painted as a thief by his family. But in the end, she thought her family would prevail, and his would say the diamond was one more thing stolen from the Foleys by the McCords.

All that between them, plus her mother's affair with his father, the child it had produced…

Don't be stupid, Paige. Forget about the man. You have to.

Because he didn't exist anywhere except inside her fantasies anyway.

She climbed into the bed. It was cold but quite comfortable. Either that or she was exhausted, if not from the previous day and night, from the emotions of this whole ordeal.

He knew who she was, and he knew what she'd come here for. Which meant she'd failed in a mission to help her family through a difficult time financially.

It was one problem her family had right now that she'd thought she could actually solve. Not the thing with her mother or Rex Foley or her brother, but the money part. She'd been willing to head into an old, long-abandoned mine alone to do it. She wasn't stupid. She'd known the risks and been willing to take it for the sake of her family.

And she'd failed.

So, the stores were in some trouble, her mother had a thing for Rex Foley, and Charlie...

Poor Charlie.

She feared she'd just made things worse for him.

Travis stretched out in front of the fire and listened to her toss and turn and sigh for as long as he could stand it, then finally turned toward her and barked out, "What is it?"

She gave a start, reminding him of the way she'd done that at each big bolt of lightning.

"Sorry," she said. "I...there's just so much, I don't even know where to start."

"You want back in the mine?" he guessed, because he knew eventually she'd get around to trying to talk him into that.

Even now, caught red-handed, she thought she could somehow charm her way back inside, thinking to steal one more thing from his family?

Unbelievable!

Women!

A man just couldn't trust them.

Just this past summer, Travis's own brother, Zane, had gone nuts over his little girl Olivia's nanny, and Travis had known right away that woman was hiding something. It hadn't taken more than a couple of phone calls to find out Melanie Grandy hadn't always been a nanny. She'd worked as a Las Vegas showgirl. Travis didn't know if Zane knew about that or not, and in the end, he'd decided to leave it alone, thinking they'd work it out. It wasn't like the woman had been a stripper or a call girl.

But now, being reminded himself of just how manipulative women could be, Travis was wondering if he'd done the right thing. He could probably use someone like Zane right now to remind him not to get stupid over a pretty, scheming woman.

"Go ahead," he urged Miss Paige McCord. "Tell me why I should let you back into that mine."

"No, it's not the mine," she insisted. "I mean…yes, I want back in it, but, no, that's not what I was talking about a second ago. It was…I wondered if I could talk to you about just one thing without…well, maybe without this whole lifelong family feud getting in the way of it?"

"Considering the fact that everything between your family and mine started there and is colored by that, I don't see how, Red."

"Yes. I know. You're right. I'm just… None of it's his fault—"

"His fault?"

"Charlie. My little brother… Your… You know about Charlie, right?"

Okay, *that* surprised him.

And *that* particular wound was still raw and festering.

He didn't really know how he felt about having a twenty-one-year-old half brother he'd known nothing about until a few weeks ago.

While he might disagree with his brothers about a lot of things, how they lived their lives, what was important to them, things like that, they were and always would be brothers. They were tight. They were family, and he'd have walked through fire for any of them anytime they needed it.

So to know that there was a fourth Foley brother out there somewhere, who'd never been one of them….

It was just wrong.

Who'd been a McCord instead.

"Yes," he admitted. "My father told us about Charlie."

His father was still reeling from the news himself. His father, steady as a rock, raise-three-boys-alone-after-his-wife-died kind of steady, absolutely reeling.

Travis didn't think anything in this world could have shaken his father like that particular bit of news.

"It's just that…Charlie's special," Paige said. "He's great. He's sweet. He's kind. He's happy. Like a puppy, just kind of silly and goofy. Everybody loves him. And he's so young. I don't…I can't stand the idea of him getting hurt in all this."

Travis got up and came to stand over her, hands on his hips, furious all over again. "And you think my father and my brothers and I are going to hurt him?"

"I don't know." She sat up in the bed, covers falling to her waist, her hair tumbling everywhere. "I have no idea how you're going to treat him or what you think

about him. I can still hardly believe it's true. That he's
your father's son and not my father's."

Travis frowned. *Okay.* He had to admit what she'd
just said was likely true, because he wasn't completely
sure how he felt about the whole thing, either. How
could anyone be? It was all too strange, too new.

"If I could just…I know you don't owe me anything,"
she said. "I know I don't have the right to ask anything
of you, but you're here and we spent some time together
before…before anything about our families got in the
way, and… Well, I think you can be a nice man, when
you want to be. And I'm asking you, please… Charlie
wants to meet your father…his father. I assume at some
point he'll want to meet you and your brothers…. Could
you just be kind? Please?"

Kind?

What the hell did she think of them? That they were
a pack of wolves? That they'd eat him alive?

And yet, he could hear that her concern was genuine
and that, for all he could see, she loved her younger
brother very much.

"Answer a question for me, Red. How did your father
treat him?"

She looked for a minute like…like it had been bad…
maybe everything Travis feared. He'd always heard
Devon McCord was an ass.

He swore, sat down on the edge of the cot and
grabbed her by the arms, holding her there in front of
him, not letting her look away. "No. Tell me. He hurt
him?" That one question burned a hole in Travis's gut
when he let himself think about it.

She looked confused, surprised, hurt herself. "No."

"The guy's always been rumored to have a nasty temper. Ask anybody, and not the people in my family who were taught from birth to hate him. Anybody. They'll tell you he was a big, tough, mean son of a bitch. So tell me. Tell me right now. Did he hit that kid? Did he hit Charlie?"

"No," she said.

"Swear it," he demanded, right up in her face. "Right now. It's… I need to know, Red. I need to know no one hurt him like that when no one in my family even knew he was a Foley, and none of us were there to protect him. Because he's family and we don't leave each other alone to face something like that. It just isn't right."

"No, he didn't hit us."

"Maybe not you or your sister, but what about your brothers? And if he knew Charlie wasn't his—"

"He didn't know," she said. "I'm almost certain he didn't. Charlie was just so easy to like. To love. For my father, too. I don't think there's any way he knew Charlie wasn't his."

"Okay." Then he realized he'd been manhandling her himself, trying to make her sit there and look him in the eye and tell him the truth.

He still had her by the arms in a hold that wouldn't allow any kind of escape from him.

And he'd gotten too close to her again.

He let his hands drop and eased back away from her as she scooted back on the bed to sit up against the headboard, looking wary and surprised and not quite sure what to do with herself or to say to him.

"I'm sorry," he said.

She shrugged off his words, like they didn't really matter, like none of it did and let her head fall until he saw nothing more than a curtain of red-gold curls and all that made him worry even more.

Travis swore and shook his head in disgust. "Did I hurt you, Red?"

"No. It's just…grabbing me like that and acting like you'd shake the truth out of me, if you had to? That was something my father did."

Her father, and now him?

That was perfect.

Just perfect.

"Son of a bitch," he said.

Now he felt like an absolute ass.

"Travis?" She put her hand on his arm. "I'm glad you care enough about Charlie to want to be sure my father didn't hurt him like that. I'm glad you want to look out for him, the way brothers do. That means a lot to me. I want that for Charlie, because I love him. And I'm glad there's at least one bit of family business we agree on. Charlie. That none of this is his fault."

"It's not. I know that," he told her.

"So maybe my family isn't as different from yours as we thought."

He scoffed at that.

Not because he thought it wasn't true, but because he didn't need to be sitting here finding common ground with her, finding reasons to like her. It was the last thing he needed to be doing.

And it didn't help any that he was sitting on her bed,

late at night, the two of them absolutely alone, with him having to keep reminding himself of exactly who she was, to keep from remembering what he'd planned to be doing with her in this cabin, in this bed tonight.

It didn't help either that he'd put his hands on her, even in anger, for a moment. And it was even worse now, when it wasn't anger that was driving him on, but the need to go to her again, this time to make sure she was okay, to comfort her, wishing he could forget everything that stood between them.

Get up, he told himself sternly. *Get up and get out of here, before you make it any worse.*

But he didn't listen.

Chapter Six

He put his hands on her again, same place as before, this time as gentle as he could be, rubbing slowly with his thumbs at the soft flesh of her inner arms. She looked wary, but she let him.

"I'm truly sorry," he said. "I don't treat women that way. It's just that…ever since I heard about Charlie, I couldn't help but worry and wonder…what it was like for him, growing up a McCord."

She gave him a look that just about had him on his knees. A look that said she understood completely and could forgive, not that he felt he deserved it.

"No one in my family wants to hurt him," Travis promised her.

She hung her head. He saw tears falling down one

perfect, pale cheek and a curtain of red-gold hair shielding the rest of her from view. She shivered a bit.

He had to remind himself he didn't get to keep her warm tonight, that the time when he was welcome to do that was long over. "What is it, Red?"

"I don't see how Charlie's ever going to belong anywhere now. Not with the way things are between your family and mine."

Honestly, Travis didn't either.

Paige shivered, and Travis had to get up or he was going to take her in his arms, despite all the reasons he'd told himself he couldn't.

He pulled the covers up around her and eased her back down onto the bed, while she looked up at him, her eyes sad and full of regrets. He let himself touch her in one small way, a hand to her cheek, wiping away those tears, and then she looked even sadder. All sad eyes and tears and that glorious hair spread out on a pillow in a bed in a cabin with him and no one else around for miles.

He wondered what she'd do if he kissed her right then, if she longed for the way it had been between them the night before. If she wished they hadn't been careful or cautious. He could have done anything to her that night, and she would have let him. He knew it.

But it was cold and wet, and the ground was hard, and she was just so soft and feminine, her body yielding completely to his. Not the kind of woman a man had on a bed of solid rock.

He'd wanted something better for her for their first time together, time, a soft bed, a fire and roof over their heads.

But mostly…time.

He'd been sure they'd have it, couldn't foresee anything that would keep them from having that time.

What a fool he'd been.

And now he'd always wonder what it would have been like, despite who she was and who her family was.

"I'm going to build up the fire. Just go to sleep. One of the ranch hands will likely come for us by midday, and we'll go to the ranch house and…I don't know, Paige. I don't know what we'll do from there. Get your Jeep for you and…I don't know."

Let her go? Just like that? No. He didn't want to do that. But what choice did he have? Forget about her? He didn't think he could.

"I just don't know," he said again, then turned back to the fire, made himself lie down and stare at it, not at her, until at some point he finally fell asleep.

Someone walked into the cabin at first light.

Travis got up, sore from a night spent on a floor that was just a tad more comfortable than the rock he'd slept on the first night, and there stood Calvin Waters, a man who'd been working the ranch since Travis was a kid.

"Sorry, Boss," he said. "You said to take care of the animals first, and we did. Just took a little longer than we thought, and then—"

He broke off as Paige rose from the bed on the other side of the room, looking all rumpled and sleepy and gorgeous in the morning light, her hair like pure fire, a curly, sexy mess.

Travis thought he heard Cal swear in utter appreciation and could have done the same himself.

Cal turned to Travis and shot him a look that said, *What the hell are you doing on the floor when you've got someone like her in the bed?*

Travis shot back his own look that said, *Don't say a word.*

Cal nodded. "I didn't bring enough horses. Didn't know you had company."

"We got caught in the storm together," Travis said. "Paige, this is Calvin Waters. He knows more about the history of the ranch than anyone, because he's about a hundred years old and I don't think he's lived a day anywhere but here. Cal, this is Paige."

He deliberately left off the last name, because that would cause a stir throughout the ranch, and he didn't want to answer any questions about her, especially since he had no answers where she was concerned.

"Hello, Mr. Waters," Paige said, giving him a polite smile.

"Oh, ma'am, it's just Cal. Glad to see you two found some shelter. It's a helluva storm out there. Let up a little this morning, but it's still miserable." Then he turned to Travis. "I only have my horse and yours. Want me to go back to the ranch and—"

"No." He wouldn't put Cal or the horses through the extra trip. "Paige and I will be fine on Murph."

He told her to get her things together and put her coveralls on. That would keep some of the rain off of her. He took care of the fire and soon they were outside.

The rain had let up, but had by no means stopped.

They stood under the narrow overhang, and the horse came up to Travis and nudged him in the shoulder.

"I think he missed you," Paige said.

"No, he's reminding me that he was smart enough to know that storm was coming and I wasn't."

Paige laughed and fussed over the horse, rubbing his nose. "Smart and beautiful, then. Good for you."

"We're going to have to ride double, and we're going to get wet one more time," Travis told her. "But at the end of this trip is a real bathtub with a huge hot water tank and it won't matter if we did lose power. We've got a generator. So you'll be warm, and you can have a hot meal, too."

"Sounds heavenly," she told him.

No, not quite, he thought, remembering that first night with her. But it was as good as things were going to get, he feared.

He climbed aboard Murph, eased back as far as he could in the saddle and then reached for her, holding out his right hand and a booted foot.

"I assume you know how to ride?"

She gave him a look of mock outrage.

"Just making sure. Put your foot on top of mine, and don't be afraid to step down hard to lift yourself up. Take my hand with both of yours, and we'll swing you up into the saddle, sideways in front of me."

"I can do it," she said. And ended up making it look easy, or maybe as if she rode double with him all the time.

It meant she was practically in his lap. He eased her against his chest, trying to ignore how that felt, and Cal handed him a blanket from the cabin that he wrapped around her. They were still going to get wet but hopefully it would offer some protection.

Cal mounted his horse and off they went, making slow but steady progress through the rain, the whole world gray and gloomy, Travis feeling that way himself, save for the fact that he had her in his arms.

It was a sad day when a man was grateful to be riding through a cold, driving rain just because it gave him one more chance to hold a woman in his arms.

But that was the shape he was in.

Grateful, despite the cold and the rain, and annoyed as hell at her whole family and his.

Paige huddled against him inside her blanket, rain finding a way to get inside, running cold down into her clothes and finding flesh. Which only made her try to get even closer to him.

She fought it. She really did.

She told herself all the reasons she couldn't have anything else to do with him, and that she really didn't know him and she shouldn't trust him. She planned that she'd be gone from here soon, and then it would be hard to believe she ever even considered…doing anything with him.

Anything else, she reminded herself. She'd already done more than enough.

It was just that, this close to him, when she closed her eyes against the misery of the cold and the rain, she tended to remember only that she was curled up against him, absorbing the heat of him, taking shelter in his arms. And despite knowing better, eventually her thoughts kept turning to that first night with him. How kind he'd been, how gentle, and how those big, hot hands of his had moved so slowly, relentlessly over every inch of her.

Teasing and teasing and teasing, until she just went mad in his arms.

Most men were in such a hurry these days. They'd forgotten how to tease and tempt and take a woman to the point where she was insane to have them.

He'd made her nearly insane with it.

The only thing that had made her wait, in the end, was knowing they would be together and that it would be all the sweeter for the wait.

How was she supposed to ignore that when she was this close to him?

He was the only thing warm in the world, his body swaying against hers, beneath hers, from the motion of the horse, his arm holding her fast, his heartbeat thudding beneath her ear. She was cold, and her whole body ached, and she just wanted to forget all of that. The memory that kept playing through her mind was of him kissing, stroking, teasing her.

"Almost there," he said, his mouth practically pressed against her ear, warm breath leaving her shivering, and not from the cold.

If she reached up and kissed him, took that warm mouth of his with hers, she wondered what he'd do. If he'd push her away or if that would be enough for her to know he was thinking of that night as much as she was, that maybe he had the same regrets, impossible as anything was between them.

She wanted him to have those regrets, she decided, pointless as that was. She just needed to know he felt the same way she did.

It is pointless, she reminded herself. *Absolutely pointless.*

The ride seemed interminable, impossible, and then finally, finally, they came to a stop.

She lifted her head and realized they were at the door to a house, his house, she suspected. He'd ridden right up to the door.

"Let me get down first, okay? And then I'll help you."

She nodded, immediately feeling the cold so much more as he lifted himself up and off the horse.

"Now, just slide down. I've got you."

She did, but her legs were numb from the cold and buckled the moment she hit the ground. The only thing that kept her from landing in a heap in the mud was him.

He caught her hard against him once more, and she couldn't even manage to help hold herself up by hanging on to him.

"It's okay, Red," he said, adjusting his grip and then lifting her into his arms.

He said something to Cal about the horses, and the next thing she knew, she was being carried inside, dripping wet, into a mudroom where a stern-looking older woman, probably his housekeeper, started fussing over her and him.

He put her down in a hard wooden chair, took off her muddy boots and sopping wet socks, took away her big, wet blanket from the cabin, then reached for the zipper on her coveralls.

His housekeeper put a big, fluffy towel into her hands and then helped her dry off her face a bit and get the worst of the moisture from her hair.

Paige's own hands were trembling so badly, she wasn't much help at all.

"Marta," he said. "Why don't you go run a hot bath in my bathroom. I'll bring her up in a minute."

He'd gotten her coveralls unzipped as far as he could with her sitting down, then took a moment to pull off his own boots, wipe the water from his face and the worst of it from his hair.

"Your bathroom?" she asked, even her voice trembling from the cold.

"Biggest bathtub in the house, Red. Looks like a fancy horse trough, but it's made of cast iron, extra long and deep. Trust me. It holds heat like nothing you've ever been in. You're gonna love it. You'll never want to get out."

She gave him a wet, weary smile.

"Come on. Up on your feet." He took her by the hand and drew her up. Her legs were kind of working again as he stripped her of her coveralls, left the rest of her wet clothes on her and lifted her into his arms again.

It wasn't necessary, she thought, fairly certain she could walk as far as his bathroom.

Still, it wasn't like she ever expected to be in his arms again.

She let her head fall to his chest once more, gave herself up to his gentle care. A few moments later, he set her down in a bathroom, big and modern and thoroughly masculine.

"We work hard here, Red," he said, as if he could read her mind. "Muscles get sore, they ache. Warm water helps."

She looked from the tub to him. She went to try to unbutton the flannel shirt she wore and mostly just fumbled with it, her hands still cold and clumsy.

He watched her do it, standing still in front of her, his face growing more and more grim with every passing second. Then he groaned and came to her, his hands replacing hers.

"I won't look," he said.

He turned her around, putting her back to him, reached around her and unbuttoned those buttons with the same no-nonsense kind of approach he might have used to undo his own shirt buttons.

He left the shirt on her, but reached up under it in back to undo her bra, then found the string tie of her borrowed sweatpants and undid them, too, while she stood there, mute, still shaking, not feeling anything but grateful for his tender, very thorough care.

He slid the borrowed pants and her borrowed boxers down a bit, then put an arm around her waist and lifted her against him and up off the floor, while he worked her pants and boxers off. Before she knew it, she was back standing on the floor in a long, flannel shirt that hung at least halfway down her thighs.

"There you go. I didn't see a thing," he said. "Think you can handle it from here?"

She nodded, then turned sideways and said, "Travis?"

He kept his eyes on her face, while she clutched the ends of that shirt together in front of her.

"Thank you."

"I'd say anytime, Red, but…well…"

"I know," she said.

"So, I'm going to walk out this door. Right now. Lock it behind me."

And then he was gone.

She locked the door with a trembling hand, slipped out of her shirt and her bra and into that blissfully warm tub.

Warmth slowly seeped into her cold body—life, heat finally.

She let her head fall back against the tub, her whole body immersed in blessed warmth.

He was right. This was a fabulous tub, about two feet deep and more than long enough for her to stretch out in. She let the tub fill almost to the brim, then cut off the water, rolled up a towel and put it over the rim to cushion her neck. She leaned back in absolute bliss and decided this was the best bath she'd ever had in her life.

She could have thoroughly enjoyed it if she had been able to think of anything but him. How kind he was mostly, how tenderly and gently he'd taken care of her, like she was the most precious thing in the world to him.

Which she wasn't. She knew it.

So that kindness, the tenderness, the care… That was just… Who he was? A part of him?

Travis Foley?

No one would ever believe her if she tried to tell anyone that. At least, no one she knew.

Yet she couldn't imagine anyone taking better care of her.

Paige let her eyes drift closed as her muscles went

slack and soft from the heat. The bathroom smelled faintly of him, a hint of spices and some indefinable thing she'd smelled when she had had her face pressed against his skin.

It was blissfully warm, the first time she'd truly been warm in days.

Her body was slowly coming back to life, her mind was filled with lazy, sensual thoughts of him. Him somewhere in this house, stripping off his wet clothes. He'd be impatient, methodical, almost mechanical, and she thought under the circumstances he'd opt for a quick, hot shower.

She groaned, imagining what he'd look like stepping into a shower, the sight of the water running down his sun-browned skin, all those lovely muscles and that dark hair on his head and his chest.

She could see his hands, lathered with soap, running impatiently up and down his body, and then see him stepping out of the shower, unselfconsciously, gloriously naked.

She wished she could be there to dry him off, taking her time, being as careful with him as he'd been with her and then pressing her body to his.

He'd kiss her hungrily, as he had that night on the ground near the mine with the storm raging, and there wouldn't be any reason to hold back.

They were safe and warm in his house, behind a locked door, and they could shut out the world if they wanted to.

She groaned, her body remembering everything.

How was she going to forget?

* * *

Travis was just outside the door, having taken a quick shower, dressed and come back with some clothes Marta had found that might fit Paige.

He'd been getting ready to knock when he heard a soft, sexy groan from inside that stopped him cold.

"Ah, God," he muttered, leaning his forehead against the closed door, thinking he could happily beat his head against the wall right now to stop thinking the things he was thinking, wanting the things he wanted.

All that subtle sexual tension of the ride here, carrying her inside, undressing without trying to do anything but simply undress her and get her into that tub so she could warm up. Honestly, he'd tried so hard to do nothing but that, to not make her feel uncomfortable in any way. And the whole time, he'd kept fighting the feeling that she was every bit as aware of him as he was of her. He'd thought that, but he hadn't done anything about it.

And now, this one, small, sexy sound from her, and he knew he was right. She felt just the same.

It had been sweet torture, having her in his arms today, having her here in his house now, in his room, in his bathtub.

He'd never be able to use the room again without thinking of her there.

"I brought you some clothes," he said. "I'll leave them in the bedroom."

"Okay," she said softly.

Then he made himself go on. "There's still a lot of work to be done around the ranch, to make sure the cattle are safe. I'm going out with some of the ranch hands. I'll probably be gone all day."

Yes, he'd just run away.

It had to be better than being here with her.

"All right," she said, like she didn't want him to leave her.

Damn.

"Just make yourself at home. There's a library off the den, all kinds of books, a spare computer that Marta uses sometimes hooked up to the Internet by satellite, if it's working right now. There's music, a TV, movies…. Whatever you want. I'll see you tonight."

"You're going to trust me, here in your house? After you caught me trespassing on your property?" she asked.

"I don't see that I have a choice. It's not like I can call the sheriff to come get you. He couldn't get here anyway, and I'm sure he has more important problems to deal with right now."

"Oh. Okay."

"And I'm more worried about the cattle and the ranch than anything you might find in this house. There really isn't anything to find that I think would help your family against mine. Much as you like to think the entire Foley clan is out to get you and your family, always hatching some new plot against you, we're not always doing that. I don't have the time, even if I wanted to. I work a cattle ranch, Red. So I'll see you tonight."

And then he had to think of a way to get rid of her somehow.

He had to get her back to her vehicle and get her off this ranch, before he did something he couldn't take back, something they'd both regret in time.

Chapter Seven

Paige stayed in that tub for a long time, letting the heat settle into her from the outside in and studying the room, all cream-colored and dark gleaming wood. Plain, masculine, yet rich and elegant.

She got out and dried herself off with a giant, fluffy towel and dried her hair as best she could considering there didn't seem to be a blow-dryer anywhere. So she put her hair in a loose braid and went out into the bedroom.

His bedroom.

Again, she found that same color scheme, cream and dark wood, a big comfy leather chair in the corner, that same clean, masculine decor.

She'd planned on trying to simply ignore the bed, not really wanting to know what it looked like, so she couldn't picture him in it. But it was on the bed that she found the clothes.

Very expensive-looking suitcases, open on the bed, all full of women's clothes.

That was interesting.

What kind of man had a house stocked with suitcases of women's clothes?

She looked over the selection in the first big suitcase.

A young woman's clothes. Young and shapely, she decided from the style and size of the clothing.

He didn't have a sister. She knew that much about the family. And none of his brothers were married. Three rich bachelors from an old Texas family did not go unnoticed. She'd have heard if one of them was off the market, although now that she thought about it, hadn't one of them been married briefly? Was it Travis? Was there some brief marriage in his past?

Paige looked through more of the clothes, many of them obviously new, still boasting their price tags. Cowgirl chic? Or someone's idea of cowgirl chic? She finally found a fairly ordinary pair of jeans she thought would fit and a white blouse, a bit frilly with its expansive, ruffled boatneck, but it would do, she decided.

She found a light pink bra she thought would fit and then wondered, if she asked, if she could have more boxers for underwear. She really didn't want to wear another woman's underwear.

But then there it was, a whole overnight case full of undies, including panties of all sorts of bright colors and varying amounts of…material. Okay, not what she would have chosen for herself, but at least they still had the tags on them, too.

She picked a pair in lavender and told herself to be grateful she wouldn't have to run around his house without panties.

There was even a makeup case.

This woman even left her makeup behind?

Paige opened it and there, indeed, was a plethora of cosmetics, scented soaps, lotions....

Had someone left in a hurry? And not bothered to come back for her things?

Paige decided to be grateful for simple things, like a good lotion to put on her face, a bit of gloss for her dry lips and—yes!—a blow-dryer. She could have dry hair.

Dressing quickly, she dried her hair and, bracing herself, opened his bedroom door and went exploring.

His was the only bedroom in this wing of the house, but there was a locked door—probably his office, she guessed—and the library with the spare computer he'd mentioned. She'd be back there as soon as she found something to eat.

The living room was huge, a massive stone fireplace dominating the space, the furniture again oversize, all buttery-soft leather and polished wood. A glance outside the big windows lining the back of the room told her it was still miserable outside.

In the kitchen, she found a pot of soup simmering, smelling wonderful, and a note. The housekeeper, Marta, said she'd left the soup for Paige and Mr. Travis. It could simmer all day and would be fine. That Paige should feel free to help herself to anything else she wanted from the kitchen and to make herself at home in the house. There was a number to call if she needed anything from Marta, who lived in a cottage near the main house, although phone service had been spotty since the storm hit.

Paige happily ate a bowl of soup, along with some homemade bread she found and a glass of orange juice, then decided she really couldn't wait any longer to call her brother, who was likely half out of his mind worrying about her. She only hoped he hadn't done anything foolish, like send someone after her, or decided to come himself.

She eyed the phone in the kitchen, but then thought if she actually got through to Blake, he'd have a million questions, and she really didn't have any answers for him and really didn't want him to know she was sitting in Travis Foley's ranch house, having gotten caught in the mine by Travis.

So she chickened out and sent him a very brief text message from her satellite phone instead.

Safe. Dry. Waiting out storm. Satellite service iffy. Phone battery low. Will call when I can. Paige.

There. She hit the send button and the message seemed to go through.

Her phone rang not five seconds later.

Blake.

Paige felt bad, but she just couldn't do it yet, couldn't tell him she'd gotten caught and that she had no idea if she could salvage anything of their plans to find the Santa Magdalena Diamond, and there was no way she wanted to tell him anything about Travis Foley.

"Sorry," she whispered, and shut off her phone. He'd

obviously gotten her message. He knew she was safe. That would have to be enough for now.

She went into the library to the spare computer, happy to find that the Internet connection, while slow and going in and out with the storm, worked well enough that with some patience she could at least see a few things.

The online weather forecast was grim. The remnants of the hurricane, now mostly just a huge blob of rain, was sitting right on top of them, stalled by a weather system moving in from the west. Massive flooding was possible. No one seemed to be sure when the two big weather fronts would end their standoff over the Texas Hill Country and the rain would move on.

Paige tried not to think about being stuck here for days.

She clicked over to the news. Her cousin Gabby's marriage to her bodyguard was still making the rounds on the gossip sites. The global market for jewelry was still down, gold prices sky high, diamonds and other gems, too. Nothing new there.

Signing into her e-mail account from online, she found multiple messages from Gabby, which she skimmed quickly.

In love. In love. Life is wonderful. In love. Where are you?

Okay, Gabby was fine, just as Paige had left her.

And then a message Paige read word for word: Where did Penny disappear to? I'm telling you, Paige, something is going on with her, and it just doesn't feel right. I think she may have finally gotten serious about a man, if you can believe that, and…well, she's just so darned naive. I'd hate to see her get hurt.

Paige would, too. And she knew her sister was very inexperienced when it came to men. Paige was the adventurous one and by most people's standards, she wasn't very experienced herself. But Penny...she was downright innocent.

Paige shook her head. She typed in a quick message to Gabby, promising to try to find out what she could, then sent one to Penny, as well.

There was a short e-mail from her mother, which Paige dreaded opening but did, just to skim.

Hope you're OK. That work is going well. Miss you. Love you. Please let me try to explain. Mom.

Okay.

More of the same from her mother, trying to explain her affair with Rex Foley.

Paige really wasn't up to that today.

She had her own Foley man to contend with.

Travis didn't think he'd ever spent a colder, wetter, more miserable day on the ranch, and mostly because he couldn't stand the idea of being in his own warm, dry house with a woman. Because he didn't trust himself there alone with her all day.

The ranch hands could have handled things easily. He knew that. They knew that. And they all knew he'd found a woman out in the storm, been stuck with her for an indeterminate amount of time and was, at first, in no hurry to be rescued. And that now she was back at the ranch and he was out here riding around in the cold and the wet with them.

They knew she was young, gorgeous and had fiery

red hair, and anything beyond that was pure speculation. But they were all speculating like mad and having a good old time of it. That he was either an idiot or that he and the woman had already had a spectacular falling-out. One or the other.

"We gonna stay out here all day or find enough sense to come in out of the rain, Boss?" Cal finally asked shortly before dark.

"Just want to make sure everything is okay," he said.

"Everything is just fine. It was fine hours ago."

Travis didn't bother challenging that notion. Just said, "I don't recall asking you to stay out here with me, old man."

"Nope, you didn't. Just hate to lose you again. I promised your grandfather I'd take care of you, and I thought I was doing a fine job keeping that promise. But if you don't even have enough sense to come in out of the rain anymore—"

"Shut up, Cal," he said.

But he turned his horse in the direction of home, and Cal followed him, not saying another word.

By the time they reached the barn and dealt with the horses, Travis was bone tired. Maybe that would be enough.

He walked into the house through the mudroom, stripped out of all of his wet clothes except his jeans, worked a towel through his wet hair as he walked in barefoot through the kitchen, as he usually did when he came in wet or muddy or both.

He nearly made it to his bedroom before he found *her,* curled up in a chair in the library in front of a roaring fire, reading a book, an image that was like a kick in the gut, it looked so…inviting.

Coming in from a long, hard day at the ranch and finding her there waiting for him. All clean and fresh and so pretty, so sexy.

She put the book down and stood up, wearing a pair of jeans and one of his ex-wife's blouses, something he actually found pretty. A creamy white against her flawless, pale skin and all that fiery hair, hanging long and loose around her shoulders. The blouse had big buttons up the front and then stopped in a scooped-out neckline that draped lovingly across the hint of curves at the top of her breasts. Her cheeks glowed from the heat of the fire and her eyes sparkled as she looked up at him like a woman who was glad to see him.

"You must be half-frozen," she said. "I can't believe you went back out into the storm today."

"Ranch work doesn't stop for anything. I have a million dollars worth of livestock out in that storm. I can't ignore that. Not for anything."

Just like he couldn't let himself ignore who she was.

"I know. I just meant…I'm glad you're back and safe."

He nodded. "I'm going to take a hot shower and get dressed."

"Marta left soup on the stove. It's delicious. And some bread I could warm up," she offered.

"Sounds good," he said, then got the hell out of that room.

Yes, she was incredibly pretty and sexy.

A day's hard ride in a cold driving rain and a tired-
ness that bordered on exhaustion couldn't change that,
he'd found.

What was he going to do now?

She warmed up the bread and dished out the soup to
him, though he told her he could manage easily himself.

"I haven't done anything all day except read and
send a few e-mails, while you were out working," she
said. It only seemed fair that she help out a little bit.
"You don't have a live-in housekeeper?"

"I don't need a live-in housekeeper. The house isn't
that big, and it's just me. It doesn't get that messy or
dirty," he said, as he poured himself a big glass of orange
juice and sat down in the eat-in kitchen. "Why? You
don't think a man is capable of surviving without live-in
help?"

"I'm just surprised. That's all," she said, sitting down
at the table with him. "You seem quite self-sufficient."

"I'm a rancher—"

"A working rancher. Not some pampered pretend
cowboy who lives in a mansion and oversees his property
and his livestock from afar."

He frowned. "What the hell kind of rancher is that?"

She laughed. "The kind I thought you would be."

"Okay, first, that is not a rancher. That's a rich wannabe
rancher. Real men despise those silly, pampered wannabes."

"Of course," she agreed.

"Just like we don't have much use for spoiled,
pampered heiresses—"

"Which I am not!" she insisted.

"No, it doesn't seem like you are."

"So, neither one of us is what the other expected," she said.

"No, we're not," he agreed, not looking too happy about it.

He finished his soup, then stood up and took his empty bowl to the sink to rinse it and put it in the dishwasher, then opened up the refrigerator and said, "Now, let's see what we have for dinner."

"Dinner? You just ate."

"That was a snack to us working men, Red."

Marta had left him a big, thick steak soaking in some kind of marinade, which he grilled himself on the stove in no time, along with a big potato he put in the microwave. When everything was done, he dug into the meal.

She stayed with him, not eating, but enjoying the company, thinking it could get lonely in a place like this, wondering about the woman who'd left all the clothes behind, if it was the isolation of the ranch that had gotten to her.

"So…the clothes? There's practically a whole wardrobe there, a lot of it things that were never even worn," she began, wondering what she could get out of him about this subject. "You just keep things around? In case women this size show up, half-drowned and with no clothes of their own?"

"Ex-wife," he told her. "When she decided she was ready to go, she went."

"Without even taking her clothes?" Paige wasn't a

clotheshorse by any means, but she couldn't imagine just walking out on a whole wardrobe, either.

"She had plenty of clothes. The woman thought shopping was a vocation."

"So, the relationship didn't end well?" she tried.

He laughed, not all that happily. "No, it did not end well."

"And you don't talk about it?" She was altogether curious about the kind of woman he'd marry and the kind who'd walk away from him.

"It wasn't a particularly enjoyable experience," he said. "What do you want to know? I met her. She was young, pretty, flirty and dressed to show off all her curves. Maybe I was blinded a bit by that. We got together fast, way too fast. Let's just say I thought she was something she was not."

And then he stopped talking.

"Something she was not?" Paige tried, hoping he'd keep talking.

"I thought she could be happy here at the ranch. Or she claimed she could, and I believed her. I live here. I work here. This is my life, and I like it. I thought I made that clear to her, but…I don't know." He shrugged. "My family has a lot of money. Women like that—"

"Men, too," she reminded him.

He arched a brow. "You're telling me you have to worry about men chasing you for your family's money?"

She nodded. "I've been fooled a couple of times."

He seemed surprised by that. Did he think women were the only ones who were manipulative enough to come after someone for their money?

"Never married?" he asked.

"No. Thank goodness."

"Well, be careful out there," he told her.

"I'm trying." Right now, she was really trying. "How long were you married?"

"One excruciatingly long year."

"And the wound is still this raw? How long has it been?"

"Three years since she left. You're going to ask if I loved her, right?"

Paige nodded. Yes, she thought she would have had the nerve.

"I think it was more that I loved the idea of her. A woman who could be happy here, share this kind of life with me and be happy. But mostly, I just felt like a damned fool in the end, and I really hate that feeling. That's the part that still burns me up. I trusted her. I believed her completely, and I'm pretty sure she just wanted a rich husband and thought she could get me to give her everything she wanted. Even if it was a life far away from this ranch."

"You don't ever want to leave this place?"

"Not if I had my way." He shrugged, then frowned and swore under his breath. "The thing is, I don't own this land, and I doubt I ever will. Your family owns it. The lease runs out in thirty years. If I ever find another woman I can trust enough to marry, to have a family with, I might be able to raise my children on this ranch, but I could never pass it on to them. I won't even be able to live my whole life here. The lease runs out when I turn sixty."

"Oh."

He said it like he'd rather cut off his right arm than leave this place.

She felt awful. She didn't care a thing about the ranch or that her ancestors and his had been fighting for a hundred and fifty years. But she hadn't thought much about the fact that the long-term lease her mother had offered as a gesture of goodwill would just give someone like Travis a chance to fall in love with the place even more before they had to give it up someday.

And it was one more reason for him to hate her family and her.

"I'm sorry," she said, knowing it was totally inadequate, but needing to say it anyway. "Maybe…maybe my family would extend the lease."

He shrugged, as if he'd absolutely hate even asking for anything from her family.

"Maybe they'd even sell the ranch to your family one day—"

"Don't say that," he told her, a hard edge in his voice that had her nearly flinching. "Not as a joke—"

"I wasn't joking—"

"Not as just an offhand comment—"

"No. I mean…I've never talked to anyone about that, never heard anyone in my family talk about it. I just…it's not like any of us has any interest in working a ranch."

He glared at her, fury in those dark eyes of his. "Just in holding on to this one, if it means keeping me and my family from actually owning it."

"No. I don't… I don't know. I'm just saying… Is this silly feud going to go on forever? Don't we all have better things to do than keep up this fight? I don't care what your grandfather did when he was young. Do you really care what mine did? It's silly—"

"When it means I can work this ranch for most of my life, but never own it, then, yes, I care. I care very, very much."

He got up and walked away, and she let him, not knowing what else she could say. If she could even make him believe she was truly sorry about what this stupid family feud had cost him…. Well, what did it even matter? It didn't change things.

He still loved this ranch and would lose it.

Because of her family.

And she knew, if it weren't for the Santa Magdalena Diamond, none of them would really give a damn about the ranch. Maybe her grandfather or her great-grandfather had, but she didn't. Her mother didn't. Her siblings… had any of them ever even been here? She didn't even know.

So, if and when she found the diamond, could she talk them into foregoing the lease and just selling Travis the ranch?

They'd think she was crazy, first of all, wanting to help Travis Foley that way. She'd never be able to explain in any way that made sense. As far as they knew, she didn't even know the man.

What could she say? He's a nice man. He loves the ranch. He's lived here practically his whole life. Why keep it from him?

And still, they'd all be incredulous and the key question

would be, Why would she want to go out of her way to help Travis Foley?

Because she wanted him.

Paige was ready to cry.

She was trained not to fall for a man who wanted her for her money, and here she was, thinking to bribe a man into falling for her because she might be able to get him his beloved ranch. That was one road to romance she'd never considered going down before. Trying to buy a man's love. What a pathetic comment on her life at the moment.

Contemplating trying to buy a man's love with the gift of a Texas ranch.

Chapter Eight

She decided she just had to get out of the ranch house, even if it was still raining. Thankfully, the horse barn was close.

Finding her boots—cleaned, no doubt by Marta—by the door in the mudroom and a slicker hanging from a hook, she took off through the rain. It had slowed, at least, but showed no signs of actually stopping.

The barn was huge, neat as could be, not ornate by any means but obviously well-appointed and not inexpensive. Travis Foley's horses lived well.

Happily for her, the place was deserted this time of night, save for the horses. She walked from stall to stall, happy to be able to walk, at least. From time to time, one of the horses got curious and stuck his head over a stall. She scratched a few long, broad noses and spoke to a few of the animals.

Travis's horse, Murph, was in the last stall on the right, and he acted as if he remembered her, giving her what for all the world looked like a smile. He tried to slip his nose beneath the hand she laid on the top of the gate to his stall, seemingly begging her to pet him.

"You big, sweet baby," she told him, obliging him with some attention.

She was still fussing over him a few minutes later when Travis walked in.

Paige took a breath, bracing herself for another confrontation with him, but when he walked over to her and the horse, he said, "I'm sorry. I know none of this is your fault."

She shrugged. "And I just wasn't thinking about you having to give up this place one day. I hope it never comes to that, Travis. That our families can come to some agreement, and you don't ever have to go."

"Thank you, but I'm a realist. I'm not holding out much hope for that."

He reached up and stroked the horse, an easy, lazy touch that had her thinking of the way he'd touched her, with a nice, slow hand that seemed to say he would take forever, just touching her. The horse looked as if he'd happily lay down his life for Travis.

She shivered, trying to put the image out of her mind.

"Going stir-crazy?" he asked.

"Just because of the rain and being cooped up inside," she said. "I'm not your ex-wife, Travis. I love the land. It's beautiful. I love being outside, riding, exploring, working the land. I wouldn't go stir-crazy in a place like this."

She would ride every morning as the sun came up, she decided. She'd explore all the old mines, just to see what they were like and imagine what it had been like to mine for silver at the turn of the century. She would know every inch of the ranch, and…

And…

She was dreaming, Paige realized.

About a life she couldn't have.

Paige shook her head and turned away from him and the horse and that life. "So, the weather forecast—"

"It's not good," Travis said.

She nodded. "I looked. I borrowed your computer and that was the first thing I checked. It could rain like this for days?"

He nodded. "We have big trucks with four-wheel drive, and we could try to get you to Llano. But we might just get stuck again—"

"No," she said. Being cooped up inside the ranch house was one thing, but she couldn't get stuck in close quarters with him again, say inside a truck or out at the hunting cabin.

"Okay. So, we'll just wait it out. That's fine. You got ahold of your family? They know you're safe?"

"I e-mailed my cousin Gabby, my sister and my mother. They didn't know I was coming here. They think I'm on an archaeology dig in New Mexico with a friend from grad school. It's just my brother, Blake, who knew. I sent him a text message today to let him know I'm safe and out of the storm, but I didn't tell him I was at your ranch house. He's going to have a million questions, and—"

She broke off and he gave her a sharp look, one that said he was just waiting for something bad to come out of any dealings with her brother, maybe her whole family.

"What is it?" he demanded.

"Blake. He's going to want to know what's going on with the search for the diamond, and I don't know what to tell him—"

"Right. There it is. You want to stay because you think you can talk me into letting you back into the mine, don't you?"

"No," she claimed.

"So, you're just giving up on the search that easily?"

"No… I just… I don't know what to do now. I don't know what to say. I didn't expect to come to your house or even to meet you. I didn't expect to get trapped with you and have some time to get to know you and now… I don't know, Travis. This is my family we're talking about. Our family's business. I told my brother I could do this, that I could find the diamond—"

"Yeah. Thrill of the discovery and all that. I remember you lying to me about it—"

"It wasn't a lie!" she cried. "Granted, it certainly wasn't the whole truth, but it wasn't a lie. I am a scientist. I like to dig in the dirt. I'm fascinated by the things created by the earth, some of them incredibly beautiful things, some of them incredibly old and still here and marvelous. And it's not easy to be taken seriously as a scientist, particularly when you're young and a woman and an heiress to a jewelry fortune. People tend to think you work as some kind of a lark. So, yes, it would be incredible for me to be the one to find this diamond. And yes, that does mean something to me. This is my life, just like this ranch is yours. How about we agree on this one thing. You don't insult my dreams, and I don't insult yours?"

"Fine," he growled. "But don't stand here and try to tell me you aren't trying to figure out how to get me to let you back into that mine, when I know you are."

"I'm telling you the truth. I don't know what to do or what to say, either to him or you. It's all just a big, damned mess, a lot more complicated than that, but that's the bottom line. I don't know what to do."

She was yelling at the end, and the horse whinnied nervously and backed away from the front of the stall, as if the crazy woman was just a little too close, and that's what she felt like. A crazy woman.

He wasn't any better, damned stubborn man.

"This isn't going to go away, just because you caught me and you run me off the ranch. You know that, don't you?" she tried, once she'd calmed down a bit.

He looked coldly furious. "Believe me, I know I'm never getting the McCords out of my life."

And that did it. It was just too much. She was too mad to even say anything. She couldn't even yell at him anymore, and if she stayed there any longer, she was going to start to cry, she feared.

So she turned around and stalked out of the barn. He chased after her.

He caught her just outside in the rain and pulled her back under the slight overhang of the barn roof, barely out of the rain.

"Ah, hell, Red. I'm sorry."

"Of course, you are."

"You just…you make me crazy, okay? You and the whole situation make me mad as hell and a little bit crazy."

"I know."

"It just doesn't seem like we'll ever really solve anything, that even trying is ridiculous, but…I don't want to hurt you, I swear. You asked me to believe you—that you really don't know what to do or say about the stupid diamond. And I do. I'll believe you about that. You believe me about this, okay? I really don't want to hurt you."

"I don't want to hurt you, either," she promised him, looking up at him through the dark with water running off her hair and her face, thinking maybe it would at least keep him from seeing her tears. "And I don't want anybody to take this ranch away from you, and I don't want…anything but good things for you. Only good."

She sniffled and then closed her eyes and shook her head.

"Ah, Red," he said, swearing as he lowered his mouth to hers and all the breath went out of her, right then and there.

That was what she'd wanted all along. Not to fight with him, but to touch him again, to have him touch her, kiss her, take her.

He gave her one, big, devouring kiss, and the current of sexual desire hummed back and forth between them, as strong as it had been that first night and every moment since in her mind.

It was as if they had their own little power source of heat and longing simmering somewhere inside of them, just waiting to be turned on.

She opened herself to him, wrapped herself around him, simply unable to get close enough to his big, hard body.

Her breasts ached. The spot between her legs throbbed. He got his hands under her rain slicker, took her hips in his hands and scooped her up. She wrapped her legs around him. It was dark and raining and no one was here. He could have her against the side of his horse barn, if he wanted. He was hard and ready. What exactly would be the problem?

Everything.

Oh, damn.

Everything that had been the problem before.

He seemed to figure it out just as she did, because he eased her back down to the ground, and his kisses went from frantic and deep and thrusting to soft and slower and slower and then…as if every touch might be the last, should be the last, and he just couldn't stand to stop.

He finally pulled his mouth away from hers, but stayed close, his forehead to hers. "You're killin' me, Red. Just killin' me."

"You're killing me, too," she said softly.

They walked back to the house, and there she was, dripping wet once again, a little cold and alone with him.

"This is a bad habit you've got," he said, taking her slicker, having her sit on a stool by the back door and getting her boots off. Then he pulled a towel out of a cabinet for her hair and refused to give it to her.

"Let me," he said. "It's one thing I think I can do without losing my head over you."

And then he started slowly, painstakingly drying off her hair.

Which made her think of being here before and in his bathroom, and him undressing her without looking at her, taking care of her and trying not to do anything else. Showing a patience and a kind of gentle caring that she had never experienced before.

Men did not take care of her. They flirted with her, they showed off for her, they challenged her, and a lot of them wanted her. But they didn't take kind, tender care of her.

She backed away from him and turned her face to the wall, fresh tears forming in her eyes.

He backed off, too, and handed her a blanket to wrap around her.

"Fire's still going in the library," he said. "Go warm up."

She nodded, then walked through his house thinking she really had to get out of here, that she just didn't know how much more of this she could take.

Wanting him and not wanting to want him. Resisting him as best she could and not wanting to resist him.

She went to the library, sat down on the raised stone hearth right in front of the fire. He came inside a moment later, poured himself a drink of whiskey and then took a seat in one of the big leather chairs nearby. All she wanted to do was crawl into his lap and kiss him silly.

She wondered for a moment if this was how her mother felt about Rex Foley and how long it had gone on—those feelings—and how long Paige could resist Travis.

Years?

Even when she was another man's wife with children of her own?

Her mother had risked everything—even her children—for Rex Foley. And Paige wondered if the son was anything like the father, if the father could possibly be as sexy and appealing.

And she owed her mother an apology, Paige realized.

She'd been angry, completely judgmental and cold toward her mother since her mother's big secret had come out, and her mother had shaken her head sadly and said, *You've never really been in love before, Paige. You don't know what it's like.*

And Paige had been horrified.

Her mother hadn't just slept with Rex Foley and had his son. She'd actually *loved* Rex Foley?

So what about Paige's father? Had her mother loved Devon McCord? And if she hadn't, why had she married him and what had their whole life as a family been about? Just Paige's father wanting to keep her mother away from Rex?

What kind of life was that for her mother?

A life of misery and longing and denial. Certainly her mother had experienced a lot more pain than Paige could possibly feel right now, after knowing Travis for only a few days.

So she showed some actual restraint, some intelligence. She got to her feet and told him she was tired and needed to go to sleep, and then she got out of that room and away from him before she could do anything even more foolish than she already had.

* * *

Paige spent a restless night, either awake and thinking about him or asleep and dreaming of him.

She didn't know which was worse.

He'd already left the house by the time she got up the next morning, having slept in a beautifully appointed guest room on the opposite side of the house from his. She showered, dressed in more of his ex-wife's clothes, and found Marta in the kitchen, a hearty breakfast of a spicy Western omelet ready and waiting for her when she appeared.

Marta had been here on the ranch with her husband, Cal, since the Foleys took over the ranch when Travis was ten, and she really didn't like Travis's ex-wife.

Oh, she didn't actually say anything about the woman, but the expression on her face while she avoided Paige's attempts at conversation said everything Marta wouldn't put into words.

Paige could not imagine Travis Foley making a fool of himself over a woman or being so wrong about one. He seemed too intelligent, too controlled to ever do that. Of course, maybe what she was seeing was the man he'd become after his marriage.

Paige, thinking she likely had another long, solitary, rainy day in front of her, went back to the library to check her e-mail.

Gabby had written back, mostly with more of the same from before. In love. In love. Gloriously in love. Where are you? And did you hear anything from Penny?

Paige opened an e-mail to reply, then set it aside,

wanting to see if she actually had heard anything from her twin first.

There it was. Penny wrote, Fine. Busy working on new designs for the stores. Where are you exactly?

Hmm.

That was odd.

It felt as if Penny was putting Paige off in much the same way Paige was trying to put Penny off, without really telling her anything of what was going on. And they just didn't do that with each other.

Okay, maybe things had been a little crazy since Paige and Blake had hatched their plan for Paige to go diamond hunting in the mine on Travis Foley's ranch, but… Well, Paige had assumed she was the only one with a big secret. She'd been happy thinking Penny was simply busy with her jewelry designs and to leave it at that.

But what if her sister was actually up to something, too?

She could probably find out… Paige could almost always find out what was happening in her twin's life. But twin intuition was a two-way street. While she was trying to read Penny, Penny would be trying to read Paige, too, if her twin caught so much as a hint of Paige trying to keep secrets of her own.

Paige wasn't sure she was ready to risk it. Not just yet.

Maybe when her feelings for Travis Foley weren't such a mess.

Which meant e-mail only for a while with her twin.

So she e-mailed Penny back, asking the same questions she'd asked the day before and gave the same answers. Fine. Working. What is up with you?

That just left her brother, and Paige feared it would

have to be a phone call today. Otherwise, Blake would likely have someone pinging her satellite phone to triangulate her position, and if that method proved precise enough to show she was sitting in Travis Foley's ranch house, her brother would have a fit over all the things she hadn't told him.

That she'd gotten caught by Travis Foley himself.

That she liked the man, wanted the man, that it was all she could do to keep from letting herself fall for him completely.

She'd promised her brother she'd find that diamond. But Travis Foley, who already didn't trust a woman as far as he could throw her, would think the worst of Paige if she tried to talk him into letting her go back into the mine to find the diamond. She could just imagine trying to explain to her brother that they had to let the diamond go as a favor to Paige, because she was losing her head over a man, a Foley man.

That would go over really well right now in her family. And yet, foolishly, that's what she wanted to do. To say, just give me this. Let's forget the diamond. I met a man. A really great man.

Right. Like she had any chance of selling her brother on that idea.

She picked up the phone in the library, sitting in that spot by the big stone fireplace she liked so much, and dialed. The line crackled, but the call went through.

Her brother answered, practically roaring, "You're at Travis Foley's house?"

Paige winced. "What?"

"You're at his house!"

"How do you know that?"

"A little thing called caller ID. It says Foley Ranch. How did you end up at his house?"

"Oops." She was so nervous about making the call, she forgot to do it using her own phone. "Blake, I'm sorry, but...he caught me."

Her brother swore.

"The first afternoon, I'm afraid. I thought I was being careful, but he was watching the mine. He saw me go in and came in after me. I didn't have fifteen minutes inside to look around before he was there—"

"Wait, he didn't hurt you, did he?"

"No—"

"Paige? Tell me—"

"No, he didn't hurt me. He's been nothing but kind to me. Not happy that we're snooping around his ranch—"

"It's not his ranch," her brother reminded her.

"Believe me, he's very well aware of that fact. But he's lived and worked here for the better part of twenty years, Blake, and he feels a strong sense of...well, he knows he doesn't own it, but... Oh, what's the point? It doesn't matter. He caught me. He knows we're after the diamond, and he's not really interested in standing by while I go back down in that mine and try to find it."

"Well, that's just too damned bad. He has a temporary lease on the land only. We own it, and if we need a lawyer or even a judge to say we also own everything on the land, I have people who'll do that—"

"Blake?" He was talking to lawyers and lining up sympathetic judges?

What a mess!

"And we never leased him the mineral rights, and my lawyer says if we want to open up the mine, to exploit the mineral rights, we have that right. Travis Foley can't stop us."

She could just see Travis's face when he found out her brother was ready to drag him in front of a judge to force his way onto the ranch and back into the mine.

"Wait," she said. "You need to be straight with me about what's going on. If you're talking to lawyers and looking for a friendly judge… How bad are things, Blake? Because I thought we might be in a tough spot financially. So many companies are these days. But now I'm starting to think it's more than that."

"I can handle it," he insisted.

"Well, I'm the one you're asking to get back into that mine, and I don't want to let you or the family down, but… He caught me, Blake. Travis Foley caught me red-handed and the last thing he wants is a big fuss with people traipsing all over this ranch looking for buried treasure that he thinks doesn't even exist. And he really doesn't want any of the McCords here."

"So talk him into it—"

Right, because she could just do that.

Talk him into it.

"Easier said than done. I mean…if we don't find the diamond, we're not going to lose the company, are we?"

It was unthinkable. McCords was a jewelry empire, respected worldwide. If you truly cared and you wanted to impress, you showed up with a pretty lavender-colored box of sparkling jewels from McCords. The family had worked for decades to build that reputation.

McCords meant flawless, high-quality stones in beautiful, artistic settings.

"Blake?" she said again, when he said nothing. "Tell me it's not that bad."

He sighed, swore once more. "Look, it's… Dad wasn't the greatest businessman. He could be impulsive at times, and he made a few bad decisions, costly decisions. When he was in charge, he was in charge. He kept a lot of information to himself, and when I took over—"

"Things were a mess," she said for him.

"I was sure I could fix it. I was fixing it, and then the whole economy went crazy. Gold and silver prices have soared, and people aren't spending the way they used to. I just… We have to have this, Paige. We have to have that diamond—"

"But even if we find it, its ownership will likely be in dispute for years, maybe decades. Legend has it that Elwin Foley was on that ship when it went down, that he got off with the diamond, and he's the one who first owned the ranch and the silver mine. The Foleys will contend that it's theirs. We'll say it's ours, and we'll be in court for years. And honestly, Blake, if that diamond truly is what legend says it is, the stone is one of a kind, a national treasure. It belongs in a museum."

"I know," he admitted. "We don't need to own the diamond. We just need to be the ones to find it."

"But all that would buy us is a few news cycles with the McCord name coupled in the press with the discovery of a huge diamond. I mean, I'm sure it would capture people's interest, but do you really think that would be enough to save the company?"

"I'm not counting on that saving the company, just making news. Big news. Capturing people's imagination, blowing the market wide open for canary diamonds."

Canaries.

Vivid yellow diamonds.

Diamonds came in all shapes and colors, but in modern times, the most prized ones were white diamonds, colorless ones actually. More recently, there'd been an increase in interest in colored diamonds, pink ones, blue ones, black diamonds. Still, it wasn't a huge market.

But the Santa Magdalena Diamond was rumored to be a huge, vivid yellow diamond, rival in size to the Hope Diamond, with a history as colorful. Some ancient legends even said the Santa Magdalena was part of a pair with the Hope Diamond that first came to fame in India, where they served as the eyes of a giant statue of a goddess. The Hope, the blue eye, the Santa Magdalena, the brilliant yellow eye, and that the people who owned them, who cheated to get them or stole them had been cursed for centuries since the diamonds were separated. In her research, Paige had even found a legend that said the curse would be broken only when the two diamonds were finally together again.

It was a fabulous story.

And her brother was right. If the Santa Magdalena, this great treasure lost for so long, was found after being hidden in the Texas Hill Country all this time, it would be a story that likely fascinated people. It was also sure to bring about a surge in interest in canary diamonds, which for a long time had been nothing but a modest part of the diamond market.

A company that skillfully positioned itself to meet that demand…

"You've been buying up canaries?" she guessed.

"I have vaults full of them," he admitted, sounding very pleased with himself.

"Oh, Blake." It was a huge risk to take, investing all that money at a time when company money was tight. But if he was right, if they found the Santa Magdalena…

"Not just that," her brother said. "Penny's been working for a couple of months on designs, Old Spanish-influenced designs, from the time when the Santa Magdalena was lost. Gabby and the PR people have a campaign that's nearly ready. We can go into production on a whole line using the canary diamonds the instant we find it."

"That's…that's brilliant."

They would own the market. There would be a huge surge in demand for a product that, in the beginning, only McCords would have.

"It had better be brilliant, because honestly, Paige, I'm afraid it's the last hope we have left. We have to find that diamond. Or…we could lose everything."

Chapter Nine

It was sheer torture to be alone with Paige in the house, so Travis went back out riding in the miserable rain, making sure he wasn't losing expensive livestock to the storm.

He was still in the barn, finishing cooling down Murph and getting him settled for the night, when Cal showed up and said his father was on the phone.

Travis swore.

Cal just laughed. "Could be worse."

"Yeah? How?"

"You can take the call in the office here in the barn."

So Travis took the call in the office in the corner of the barn, with Cal laughing at him as he walked in to do it.

"Travis?" his father said. "Glad I finally got through. Everything okay there? The storm looks nasty."

"Yeah. Just a little water, a little mud. We're fine, Dad."

"Good. The flooding on TV looks massive. I'm glad it hasn't been bad this far north."

Travis sighed. "It's big, but we have high ground, too, and we haven't lost any cattle yet. So far, it's just cold and wet and damned annoying."

"I'm sure you're handling the situation just fine, son," he said, sounding tired, Travis thought, maybe even troubled.

"Dad, are you okay?"

"I am. I thought…well, I'm not sure if you want to know this, and I realize it's still a shock. It's still one to me, too, but…Eleanor's son…my son…Charlie decided he was ready to meet me."

"Oh."

"Yeah. I didn't want to rush him. I mean, if I'm fifty-eight and a father three times over already, and I don't know the half of what I feel about this, how's he supposed to know at twenty-one? So I promised Eleanor I'd wait until Charlie was ready, and finally, he was."

Wow. His father actually sounded shaken, vulnerable.

It was something Travis didn't think he'd ever heard in his father's voice or ever would.

"So, you saw him already? How was it?"

"It was—"

His father broke off. Silence came through the line for a moment, and then his voice broke, he sighed painfully.

Was his father in tears?

A man who'd raised three young sons on his own after his wife died? A man Travis had always considered as strong and solid as a rock.

"Dad?"

"Sorry, I… Damn. He's a great-looking kid," his father insisted, laughing and, Travis suspected, doing his best to cover up anything else he was feeling. "I mean, he's my boy. Good-looking, like all my boys, solid as a rock, strong, smart, plays a little football. Great kid. Has no idea what he thinks about me and our whole family, but…just a great kid."

"That's good. I'm glad, Dad."

"Really? You mean that?"

"Yeah, I do. He's a Foley. He's one of us, no matter what else he is," Travis said. Plus, he'd promised Paige he'd smooth the way as best he could for Charlie with the rest of his family, and he was a man who kept his promises.

"Thank you, Travis. It means a lot to me."

"Sure. And…I want to meet him, whenever he's ready." One of the horses started acting up, making a racket, reminding Travis of one thing they could all do together. "Maybe he'd like to come to the ranch one day. You and me, we'll put him on a horse and see what he can do. How about that?"

"That…that sounds great."

"So, you want to tell him? Or do you think I should? I'll do whatever you think is best."

"Well, I'm not sure. I'll let you know," his father said, then hesitated for a moment. "Actually, Travis, what I'll do is ask Eleanor how she thinks we should handle that."

Eleanor?

Travis sat up straight in the office chair, not sure if he liked where this conversation was going. "Okay."

"I'll ask her tonight, when I see her."

Oh.

So, was Travis supposed to ask? Did he really want to know? In the end, he decided he did want to know. "You're seeing her?"

"Yes."

He swallowed a curse. "Dad, I thought you were furious at her for having your son and keeping it from you all these years?"

Travis was, and he knew damned well his father had been in the beginning.

"I was," his father admitted. "But I'm not blameless in this situation—"

"Blameless? You didn't know for twenty-one years that you had a fourth son out there in the world."

"No, but I knew she was married when we were together, and I knew what we were doing was wrong. But I ignored all that because…well, Eleanor and I… There was a time, a long time ago, when I was just crazy in love with her, and she ended up with Devon McCord. But I never forgot her."

Jesus, Travis really didn't want to know this. None of it. Because it brought up a million questions he really didn't want answers to, either.

He hardly had any memories of his mother, but from all he'd heard and what little he did remember, he would have sworn she was a kind, loving, happy woman. Travis really didn't want to hear that his father had never loved her, had spent his whole life in love with Eleanor McCord and wishing he could have her, instead.

What the hell kind of life was that?

"I loved your mother," his father continued, as if reading Travis's mind. "I truly did. She was a wonderful woman, a wonderful mother, and she loved you and your brothers dearly. We were happy together, Travis. I couldn't believe it when I lost her. I felt in some ways I had cheated her, just by having those old feelings for Eleanor, even though I never acted on them while your mother was alive. I promise you that. I hope you believe me. It was only after your mother was gone that…"

"Dad, really, you don't have to—"

"No, I want you to know. I'm sorry. It was wrong, and I knew it. When Devon left Eleanor, she thought their marriage was over, and I thought we were going to get our chance. Then Devon came back and she had to make a choice."

"And she chose him?" How could she choose Devon McCord?

"She chose to protect her children, and that meant going on with the marriage. I know it wasn't easy for her, but…Travis, when you have children, things change. Their needs become more important than yours. You'll have children of your own one day, and maybe then you'll understand what she did."

"And you're going to just forgive her for that? For having your son and keeping him from you all those years?" Because Travis didn't understand that at all.

"Not easily, but I'm damned sick and tired of living without her. I can tell you that. She's here now, and her children are grown and it's time we got to think about ourselves and not anyone else. I'm sorry if that hurts you, or if you don't understand. But Eleanor and I are going to be thinking about ourselves now and what we want."

"Good God, you're still in love with her?"

"I never stopped loving her."

Travis slumped back in the office chair, feeling like the earth had just shifted beneath his feet.

His father was in love with Eleanor McCord? He couldn't even imagine how the ripples of that relationship were going to move through their world. Not easily. That was for sure.

And no easier for the woman inside his house right now.

Paige calmed herself down, thought things through and then decided that one way or another, she had to talk Travis into letting her search for the diamond. She had to. Her family's business depended on it.

And she didn't even think she could tell him that. Which meant…well, she didn't see how she'd make him understand.

So she paced and went over everything she'd figured out about the diamond and its possible location and about the Eagle Mine, and then she paced some more.

The day passed with excruciating slowness, and if the rain didn't stop soon, she was going to scream. By the time she heard Travis come in that evening, she was sitting on the big sofa in the living room trying to scrub her face free of tears that had fallen a while back, hoping it wouldn't show.

He looked surprised to find her where she was, sitting in a dimly lit room, wrapped up in an afghan, seemingly doing nothing at all. But he was wet and tired and no doubt cold, and off he went to shower and change.

She was still sitting there when he came back, and that time, he walked into the room and stopped talking midsentence as he caught sight of her.

Carefully, he came to sit beside her on the sofa, close but not too close, taking her hand in his.

"Let me guess," he said finally. "You talked to your mother?"

That brought her head up to face him. "What's wrong with my mother?"

"Nothing." He looked confused then.

"No. What did you hear?" God, what else could have gone wrong? Her family's business was near to going under, and her mother? What had her mother done?

Travis shrugged. "I figured it had to be a family member. Mother, brother, sister. I took a shot. So, which one was it?"

She hung her head miserably, still trying to figure out exactly how much she could tell him, how she could explain and get him to let her back into the mine without hating her.

"Okay, Red, the thing is, it's hard enough seeing you look this miserable, when I'm just looking for an excuse to touch you. And I'm telling you right now, you start to cry, and that's it. I won't be able to just sit here and do nothing."

"Promise?" she asked.

He nodded.

And she let those tears fall.

He swore softly and scooped her up and onto his lap,

pulling her down against his chest and wrapping her up in those wonderful arms of his.

He didn't even try to tell her to stop or that everything would be okay or that it couldn't be that bad, which she appreciated very much. He just held her and let her cry, tears rolling slowly down her cheeks, misery pouring out of her.

His body was big and hard and warm, and he smelled so good, fresh from the shower. She laid her head on his shoulder and eased into that spot where his shoulder met his neck, one hand pressed flat over his beating heart, letting the comfort and the reassurance of him seep into her.

"Do you ever just want to run away from your whole family and all of its problems and go somewhere where no one can find you?" she whispered.

"Not me. I'd find a way to seal the borders of this ranch and cut it off completely from the outside world. No one would get in without my say-so. That's my idea of paradise when they're all driving me crazy."

Paige grinned. "Okay, do it. That would work."

"Red, the thing is, I just haven't figured out how. But if I did, I'd keep you inside with me, and I wouldn't let anybody from your family in, either."

Which made him her hero.

She let her hand slide up to the side of his face, and snuggled deeper into the curve of his shoulder. How could a man be so comforting and yet so sexy at the same time?

"What do they want you to do, Red?" he asked finally. "Get back into the mine? Is that it? Talk me into it? No matter what it takes?"

She nodded.

"Well, they sure knew the right person to send," he claimed. "If anybody could talk me into it, it's you. You could probably talk me into anything."

"I don't want to do it," she tried to explain. "I want you to understand that. To believe it, if you can. I don't want to do that to you. To use…this thing between us just to get back into that mine."

He took a breath, a slow, deep steadying one, let one of his hands stroke her hair. "But you will anyway?"

"I have to," she said.

He eased her away from him just enough that he could look her in the eye. "No, honey, you don't."

"I promised I'd do whatever it takes to get back into that mine and find the diamond—"

"Whatever it takes?"

She nodded.

"Fine," he said. "Tell your family the price of entrance is you in my bed. See how they like that."

She laughed sarcastically. "I wish it was that easy. You could be the evil Foley man who used me terribly, and I'd be the self-sacrificing heroine of the story who gave up her body to the evil one for the good of her family."

"You make me sound like a complete cad, Red."

"Only to my family. To yours, I'd be the scheming woman who was willing to use her body to seduce you into getting what my family and I wanted."

"Oh, well. In that case…it's a brilliant plan," he agreed.

"It is. Both our families would understand."

He rubbed his cheek, slightly rough with late-day

stubble, against hers. "And we'd get what we want anyway. We'd get each other."

"And our families would have one more reason to hate each other."

"Yes, they would," he said, pulling her closer, his hold one of comfort and admirably restrained desire. "You know, I feel compelled to point out that we don't ever have to tell anyone what we do on this ranch. No one would ever have to know. Have you thought about that?"

"Yes," she admitted.

"And if no one ever knew, who could it possibly hurt?" he reasoned. "Just you and me. If we…came to care enough about each other, or if just one of us cared enough…"

They could get hurt.

She started crying again. He had a hand on the side of her face, pressing her close, and he felt those tears, swore softly and then he was kissing her, slowly, deeply, hungrily.

Nothing more.

Just kissing her like he wanted to devour her right here on the sofa.

She sank into him, into the pleasure, going boneless in his arms, wanting to be nowhere else but there. Her heart started thudding heavily, her body warm and tingly all over, the pleasure centered on the point where his mouth was joined with hers, as if every sensation, every bit of energy, of life sprang from that union.

Take me, she wanted to beg him. *Take me so fast I don't have time to think or to pull away. Just do it, and we'll worry about the consequences later.*

He rolled them in one smooth motion, and she ended

up flat on her back on the sofa with him on top of her, his body all big and hard and ready.

She loved the feel of him there, the weight of him, the heat, the way one of his thighs slipped between hers in an intimate promise of the pleasures in store for them both.

He made short work of the buttons of her shirt, undoing only as many as it took to allow him access to one breast. He pushed her bra aside and there was no teasing this time, just him sucking hard on her nipple, the sensation opening up a line directly to that place between her thighs and setting that spot to throbbing.

She wanted her jeans off, wanted his off, wanted his mouth... She wanted it everywhere, right then, no more waiting.

She'd come right then and there, if he kept sucking on her nipple that way. Just that would be enough.

He slid his thigh high against her, stroking her through her jeans, and she arched up against him, holding his head to her breasts.

The man made her insane.

The whole situation was insane, but he was right.

No one would ever have to know.

It was their lives, their bodies, their secret, their time out of time, right here, right now.

Paige had this crazy impulse to tell him she loved him. It flashed through her head in a second, taking her breath away, leaving her weak and scared and thrilled, all at the same time. Did she love him? She had never really felt that way about anyone before.

He moved from one breast to the other, and she made

a purring sound of pure pleasure, pure need. Now he was messing with her mind as much as her body.

She'd be crazy to even think of loving him.

Still, the idea kept nagging at her, running around in her brain, sneaking through the fog of pleasure he'd created there and making her actually think about it.

What if she loved him?

And then when they finished this, and she had to talk him into letting her go find the diamond…he'd think this was all about that damned diamond.

"Dammit," she muttered.

He lifted his head for an instant, annoyed and breathless and so sexy it hurt. "What?"

"I…I'm sorry, but we can't do this yet!"

He groaned, closed his eyes, hung his head over her chest, the rest of his body still lying heavily on top of hers.

"We just…we have to settle this thing with the stupid diamond first, Travis. I'm sorry, but we do."

"We already did," he complained, but he rolled off of her anyway.

Travis pulled her up on her side with her back against the sofa, and he rolled onto his side, too, facing her. He looked seriously annoyed, seriously aroused.

"You're going to sleep with me, so I'll let you look for the diamond, remember? And I'm going to let you seduce me, and then I'll be so crazy for you, I'll let you do anything, including look for the diamond. It's perfect and both our families will understand, because they expect the worst of each other, anyway."

"I know, but that's for them, if they ever find out and

start being jerks about it. I'm talking about us. We have to settle this first for us because…because…"

"Because why, Red?" He cupped her face with his hand, still breathing hard but giving her a sweet smile.

"Because I couldn't stand it if you thought I was going to sleep with you to get that damned diamond," she said.

He looked completely exasperated. "At the moment, I don't really care why you do it, just that you do."

"I know, but come morning, you will care and I'll care, too. I can't have you hating me, Travis, or thinking I'm just another scheming woman who wants something from you and will use her body to get it."

He sighed, then swore. "I don't think that."

"Maybe not now, but afterward, when I start talking you into letting me back into the mine, you will. So we have to settle this now, and then…we can do whatever we want."

He went still, really looking at her. "Promise? The we-can-do-whatever-we-want part? After we settle this?"

"Yes. And my vote for what happens right after we settle this would be getting naked."

"And you expect me to have a serious conversation with you after hearing that? I hardly have any blood in my brain right now, Red."

"Come on, focus. We have a goal in mind, Travis. We settle this, we can get naked."

He shook his head, trying to clear it. "If this is your idea of negotiating, you're really good at it."

"This is me, sick of everything standing between us and wanting to fix it, so I can take my clothes off and climb into your bed. Come on. Get up. We can't do this horizontally, and I think I have an idea."

Chapter Ten

He sat up, got to his feet, poured himself a shot of whiskey neat and ran a hand through his hair, thinking if she was out to mess with his head, she was succeeding brilliantly.

Maybe he was a fool, but he really didn't care, because he was going to have her. And maybe then he'd be able to think straight and make some sense of this whole thing.

Maybe.

He sat back down, on the far end of the sofa, and she sat at the other end, turned sideways to face him, one leg tucked up under her, her arm stretched out along the back.

God, he loved that wild, crazy hair of hers.

That was his first thought. Not the greatest start to any negotiations, he knew, but still… That hair was magnificent. It made him absolutely crazy. He wanted it spread out over his chest after they made love, could imagine her stroking his entire body with her hair.

"I don't think you're focusing," she said.

Travis rolled his eyes, telling himself she wasn't his ex-wife, and he wasn't about to get stupid over a woman again. The thing was, she was so much smarter than his ex-wife and more beautiful, and he wanted her even more.

Which had the potential to make him even stupider and her even more dangerous, which was a terrifying thought.

God help him.

"Okay, Red," he said. "Tell me why I'm going to let you back into that mine. I'm assuming you have some reason other than the fact that you're gorgeous and sexy, and I want you so bad I can hardly see straight?"

She blinked up at him. "You're not helping. Focus, remember?"

"Okay, tell me why."

"Because my brother is as stubborn as you are, and he won't give up trying to force his way onto the ranch, just because you say no the first time or the first ten times he tries to make it happen. And the whole thing will just turn into one giant hassle that goes on and on, and you'll hate that, Travis. You'll absolutely hate it."

"Yeah, I would, but that's no reason to give him what he wants," he argued, hating her brother right now. "And what the hell is wrong with the guy? Sending his little sister in to do a dangerous job like heading into an abandoned mine? I plan on telling him that, too."

She frowned. "When you have a geologist in the family, someone who actually has experience working in mines, if you're smart, that's who you send to do the job. And you're not staying focused."

"Okay. Fine. But I have to say, the idea of frustrating your brother sounds really good to me."

"Not if that's not what you really want. Think about yourself here and what you want—"

He grinned. "That's easy, Red. I want you."

"Besides me. You want as little hassle as possible with my family, especially over the diamond, which is probably here on this ranch you love. Think about it. No more treasure hunters sneaking onto your ranch, and no McCords taking you to court, if they have to, to get into that mine."

"Court?"

"Stubborn, Travis. Remember, my brother's very stubborn, like you. And, as he's already pointed out, my family owns the mineral rights. We're talking about a mine. He claims we have the right to go in there and mine anytime we want. He'll say we're simply exercising the mineral rights and we can fight in court, if you want, for a long time. But you don't want that. What do you want?"

"Besides you naked? Right?"

"Yes, besides that. Come on. What do you want? You want to never have a hassle over this stupid diamond again, right?"

He blinked once, then again. Absolutely damned right. "Yes. How do I get that?"

"By settling it right now. You and me. We'll do it together. All we have to do is trust each other a little."

He balked at that.

"I know. Not your strong suit. Stay with me here. You

trust me, at least a little bit, right? And I trust you. I want a chance to look for the diamond, and you get a chance to get my brother off your back."

"Only if you find the damned thing. If not we'll be looking forever. There are five old silver mines on this ranch."

"But there's only one that matters. The Eagle Mine. I…I'm trusting you, Travis. We have the original deeds to the silver mines. There's a clue on one of the deeds. A tiny clue on the border to the deed to the Eagle Mine. There's a tiny diamond in one of the eagle's claws. There's nothing else like that on any of the other deeds."

He frowned. "Pretty thin as clues go."

"Your grandfather Elwin Foley was on that ship when it went down. He was the first owner of this ranch. My grandfather Harry McCord is the first one to have a deeded ownership of that silver mine. If Elwin hid the diamond here, and Harry found it after he won the ranch from Elwin, Harry wouldn't have left it there without some kind of clue about where he hid it. He must have been hoping that one of his ancestors would find it later and be able to claim it as his own, with no challenge from Elwin Foley."

Travis was skeptical, but she seemed to believe she knew where that diamond was.

"That mine is full of petroglyphs," she reminded him. "You know that. You let the archaeologists inside the mines last year. I have their final report, cataloging the drawings and carvings. Eight of the petroglyphs in the Eagle Mine are of eagles. Don't you see? The diamond is in the Eagle Mine, the spot marked by one of the eagles."

Damn.

Maybe she would find it.

"And if I don't find the diamond," she continued, "this whole thing will be over in a week or two. I'll go to my brother and tell him the diamond's not there, and he'll believe me. And he'll have no reason to ever bother you with this again. You'll have all the peace and quiet you want."

Travis had to admit, that part sounded good.

"I'll even tell the world we know where Elwin Foley left the diamond, that Harry McCord found it and marked the spot, but it's not there anymore. That we looked, and that someone must have already found it. I'll look exhausted and like I'm ready to cry. I'll trot out all my academic credentials and even show them the clue on the deed. People will believe me, and they'll all leave you alone again."

Travis frowned. Either he was still all caught up in getting her into his bed as quickly as possible, or that made sense. He really did just want the whole mess with the diamond to end. Still, it had been so long since he trusted any woman, and he hated feeling like a fool.

"Travis, this is like the whole thing with the ranch. You don't really care about the diamond. You just don't want my family to have it. And my family doesn't really care about the ranch anymore. They're just too stubborn to want you to own it. Do the right thing here. Do the thing that causes you the least amount of hassles and forget about the rest."

"Forget that your family is getting what it wants," he reminded her.

"Just remember that you're getting what you want. Oh, hell, you think we're all crazy to believe the diamond's even there. I can tell. So if you're convinced we're not going to find anything anyway, then this is just sheer stubbornness on your part, to not want to let any of the McCords look for it."

"Well," he conceded, "the Foleys have been accused of being stubborn before."

"Yeah, I've heard that. Come on. You know everything I just said makes sense."

Damn, it did.

He was almost certain it did.

"I know what you really want is the ranch," she said, "but my brother doesn't own it. I can't get you the ranch from him, but when this is over, I'll talk to my mother. I'll do everything I can—"

"Red—"

"I know. You don't think it will ever happen."

"No," he admitted. "I don't. I accepted that a long time ago."

But he made her want to believe it was possible.

"I'm going to do everything I can," she said.

Like she thought she could do anything in the world.

He shook his head, thinking she was still a McCord, and he was half-blind with wanting her, no doubt not thinking clearly.

"And then, there's the fact that I'd have to stay here until it stops raining," she said, giving him a purely wicked smile. "And it's flooded everywhere. I'd have to wait until the water went down, so I could get to the mine, right? Night after night?"

"Okay, now you're just messing with my head," he said, thinking about nothing but her naked again.

She grinned that super sexy grin of hers. "And…we don't know, but the mine might be flooded underground, too. I'd have to wait for the water to go down there, and then I'd have to have time to search…."

"And you'd spend every night of that time in my bed," he said, not asking her, telling her. "How is this different, exactly, than you sleeping with me to get to the diamond?"

"If I was going to do that, I wouldn't have made you stop a minute ago. This is the two of us having a rational discussion about an issue between us and coming to a rational solution to that problem. So we can put it aside and think now of nothing but ourselves and what we want."

Okay. He supposed he got the distinction.

He still felt fuzzy-headed from wanting her so badly, but he thought she'd made sense in all her arguments.

He just had one reservation. "It's not just stubbornness on my part to want to keep you out of that mine. I worry about you, Red. I can't stand the idea of you getting hurt down there or God forbid, trapped in there. I'd never forgive myself."

"We'll do it together. We'll be careful. I promise. I know how to do this, Travis, and I'll have you with me. I couldn't let anything happen to you, either." She grinned. "So, we've agreed?"

He nodded. "Yes. Now take your clothes off, Red."

"Here?" she whispered tentatively.

He was halfway out of his shirt and kicking off his boots at the same time. When he actually got the shirt over his head and tossed it aside, boots off, he looked over at her, standing hesitantly by the sofa.

"Yes, here," he grinned. "Is that a problem for you?"

The fire was going, and they hadn't turned on the lights as darkness had fallen outside, so the room wasn't brightly lit by any means. And there was a nice, soft rug in front of the fire.

She looked incredible by firelight.

He already knew that from their time in the cabin.

"Anybody could just walk right in here," she protested.

"Has anybody done that in the evenings since you've been here?"

"No," she admitted. "But—"

"Are you nervous, Red?"

"A little."

"Shy?" he tried, wondering if she could possibly be that. He'd had her nearly naked on the ground the first night they'd met, after all.

And what a night that had been.

He'd made her crazy. He'd made sure of it. Absolutely crazy, more than once, enjoying the way she responded so openly, with such honesty and abandon. Wanting her so crazy for him that the minute they got anywhere with a condom, he could be inside of her, no questions asked, no hesitation, no nothing.

And it hadn't quite happened like that, but he'd been carrying a condom in his pocket ever since they got to the cabin, like some damned teenager thinking he might get lucky any minute. Someone had been using the cabin as a love nest. He'd found the condom stash there.

"I'm not..." she began. "Just...I didn't think...."

He took her by the hand, led her to stand in front of him as he sat and told her, "Don't worry. I'll take care of everything."

He started at the bottom button of her blouse, pulling it open, putting his mouth to that spot on her belly near her belly button, his arms wrapping around her, hands cupping her bottom, pulling her to him.

She whimpered, grabbed his shoulders, had her hands in his hair.

"There you go," he muttered against her soft, trembling skin. "It's gonna be just fine. Did you like what I did to you that first night at the mine, Red?"

"Yes," she whispered.

"So we both know that I already know what you like, right?"

"Yes."

"You'll like this even better. Trust me."

She did. She trusted him.

And then his tongue slid around the opening of her belly button and then ever so softly inside.

Her muscles went slack, legs just gone, and it was only his arms holding her tight and the way she draped herself over him that held her up.

That wicked tongue of his…

It felt for all the world like he was inside her, really inside her. Heat blossomed in her pelvis, blood thrumming through her veins, until he dragged her back onto the sofa with him, facing him, straddling him, laughing.

He held her with one hand, undid buttons up her blouse with the other, that wicked mouth following, like he might lick every inch of her with a hot, sensual slowness and make her insane.

He got to her bra, which happened to close in front and flipped it open, nosed the cups aside again, there was that mouth, those little licks of wet heat, under her breast, around it, that ultrasensitive outer curve and then finally he took her nipple in his mouth and sucked hard.

She arched against him, felt him, hard and ready, against her through their clothes. She didn't care anymore that they were in his living room, that anyone could walk in or that it wasn't quite dark in the room.

He went from one breast to the other, and one hand went to the snap of her jeans, the zipper, and then to his own. A moment later, he palmed her hips and stood up, taking her with him. Then he put her on her feet, just long enough for him to strip her of her jeans and panties, then strip off his own, as well.

She didn't think she'd ever felt so naked in her entire life as she did when he sat back down and just gazed at her standing there in front of him, a look in his eyes that dared her to object or to try to cover herself. Her breasts ached with fullness. Her nipples were so tight, and she was absolutely throbbing with desire.

"Red, you're beautiful," he said in that slow, sexy, cowboy drawl of his.

Then he reached out and teased at the patch of red curls between her legs.

"Travis, you can't do that," she objected.

"Do what?" he said, watching as she reacted to his touch.

"Leave me standing here like this."

"But I can see you like this, all of you, and I already told you, you're so beautiful. I love looking at you like this," he said, as his wicked fingers slipped inside those curls.

She grabbed on to his shoulders in an effort to stay upright.

This could not go on. She wouldn't be able to stand it.

Sensation shot through her, wave after wave of it, the touch simply too much to bear. Not that it stopped him. He kept right on going, with her begging him, telling him he just had to stop.

But he didn't.

He kept going until she groaned, then gasped, nearly screamed.

"Now that might actually make someone come inside, if anyone was close enough to hear."

He was laughing as he pulled her onto his lap and wrapped her up in the afghan from the back of the sofa.

She would have yelled at him, but she still couldn't talk, still had waves of pure pleasure shooting through her body. She let her head fall to his shoulder, and with her legs splayed wide this way, she could feel him, throbbing hard against the slick opening of her body, and she rocked against him ever so slightly, because she just couldn't help herself.

Oh, it felt so good.

He felt so good.

"If someone comes in here, I'm going to kill you," she told him.

"You're covered up, and even if they do come inside, they won't stay long."

"Travis!"

He laughed again. "If they were close enough to hear you, they'd have been here by now to make sure everything was okay. So you're safe, Red. And you're not going anywhere."

She arched against him and rocked, using him to please herself now and hoping that would make him a fraction as crazy as he'd made her.

He groaned, a sound she took as encouragement, and then he had his hands palming her hips, finding a rhythm he liked.

She nipped on his ear, teased at it a bit, remembering what he'd done to her belly button, then rubbed against him some more, whispering, "Feel what you did to me. It felt so good. You feel so good."

He growled deep in his throat and pushed her away. She sat back on his lap, puzzled until she realized he had a condom and was putting it on, then pulling her back to him.

She started out high on her legs, fitting her body to his and then let him slowly ease her down around him, letting him slowly open up her body and fill it with him. He was big and hot and throbbing, and she felt her body grip him, squeeze him tight, as if she'd never let him go.

It was too much, too sweet, too hot, too much to control, so she just hung on to him and let him do it, let him set the rhythm with his hands on her bottom, that sexy voice of his urging her on, take him, take more, take him deeper.

She whimpered, protested, buried her face in his hair, and he finally flipped her over onto her back on the sofa and came down hard on top of her, rocking into her in a maddening rhythm, so steady, only so deep, only so hard.

He was trying to kill her, she decided.

Kill her with pleasure.

"What?" she cried. "You want me to beg you to finish it? Is that it?"

"Yes," he said, wicked man. "I think I would like that."

But he didn't make her, he laughed deep in his throat and finally let go of all efforts to control this thing between them or to prolong it.

And then it didn't take anything at all.

She'd been hanging on that edge for what seemed like forever, and he finally pushed her over it. She buried her face in his shoulder, to muffle the sounds she made and felt him surging into her, her body milking every bit of pleasure out of his.

It was amazing. It was beautiful, and it was so much more than she'd ever felt before.

He was a magic man, she decided.

Beautiful, sexy, strong, with a control streak a mile long, but she didn't care. She just gave herself over to the sheer pleasure of finally having him in every way that mattered.

Paige knew that at some point, he rolled heavily off of her, wrapped her in that afghan and carried her to his bed, sliding her between the cool, soft sheets and then covering her up.

She grumbled about the cold.

He laughed. "Give me a minute, Red. I'll be happy to warm you up all over again."

"No," she said. "I need a week, maybe two, to recover from that."

She wasn't sure she could move her own legs or her arms, her whole body was so heavy and so relaxed, it was limp with pleasure.

"A week?"

He was back, standing naked by the bed, condoms in hand.

She looked at him, giving him a slow once-over as he'd given her, except here in his room it was darker.

Still, she could see enough to appreciate the sight.

He pulled back the covers and got in, put on another condom and rolled onto her.

"Travis," she protested, wanting him all over again, just too sated to do anything about it.

"We'll go easy this time, Red. If anything can ever be easy with us," he whispered as he slipped inside her still-aroused body.

Just like that.

Easy as could be.

A million sensations came thundering back, making her whimper and open herself up to him even more.

It was pointless to protest.

She'd give him anything he wanted right now, she realized.

Anything.

Paige woke up to find him looking at her again.

She was in his bed, and it was morning, or nearly morning, judging by the faint light coming in the window.

He was lying stretched out beside her, propped up on his side. He'd pulled the sheet down to the top of her thighs and was stroking her slowly. His hand skimmed just above the surface of her skin, a touch more implied than anything else, and it was as if her body was rising up to meet his hand, begging him in its own way to touch her.

"You are a wicked man," she said, her hand on his cheek, wanting him to kiss her. "And you need to shave. Your skin is rough."

"All the better to rough you up, my dear."

She laughed as he did just that, rubbing his chin against her belly, her breasts, her cheek, taking her back, just like that, to that heated pool of desire between them.

How did he do that?

It was like it was always there, simmering, just ready to boil over.

He kissed her once, then again, then studied her face, touching her cheek, tracing a path around her mouth. "I'm afraid I roughed you up a little bit last night, honey. Your skin is reddish. Is it sore?"

"A little," she admitted.

"What me to shave?"

She shook her head, pulling his mouth down to hers. "I don't want to wait."

"You're gonna be sore in other places, if we're not careful," he said.

"Maybe, but I don't care."

The next time she rolled over, she must have been dreaming. Because something that looked for all the world like morning sunlight was shining in through the bedroom window.

Paige blinked once, then again.

It had been days since she'd seen anything resembling sunlight.

It was like waking up to a completely different world.

So was finding herself naked in Travis Foley's bed.

Paige took a breath, pulling the air in as deep as she could and very, very slowly letting it out.

She'd become his lover, and she wasn't sorry.

She was glad, very, very satisfied and a little bit sore.

The man was insatiable. Wonderfully so. She'd never had a lover so sure of what he wanted and the fact that he was going to get it. It was maddening, and, though she hated admitting it even to herself, really turned on. As if he planned to turn her into his personal love slave, and she'd do it, because he made her feel so good.

She was contemplating actually getting up, maybe soaking in that fancy horse trough of his to get some of the soreness out, when he walked in, dressed this time.

Paige glanced at the clock. It was after nine. He was never home at this hour.

"Back for more?" she asked, thinking this whole love slave thing had gone to his head, too.

He grinned, shook his head and held out the phone she hadn't noticed him carrying to her. "It's your brother."

She gaped at him as he clamped a hand over the earpiece. "No!"

"Afraid so, Red. Sounds like he keeps close tabs on you, didn't like it when he hadn't heard back from you first thing this morning."

Horrified, she looked at the phone like it might jump up and bite her. "You didn't… He doesn't…"

"No. Of course not. And he can't see through the

phone, so he has no way of knowing you're naked in my bed, so try not to look so worried. Or sound so worried. He sounds like he already believes I'd throw you to the wolves if I had the chance."

She took a breath, sat up to lean back against the leather headboard and lost track of the sheet in the progress, having to scramble to cover her breasts once more.

"This is impossible!" she complained.

And then he shoved the phone at her, and she had no choice but to say, "Hello? Blake?"

"What has that man done to you?" her brother practically roared.

Paige fought down a near-hysterical chuckle and motioned for Travis to come back into the room, when he started leaving. She didn't have anything to hide anymore, except bare breasts, at least for the length of this phone call, if she could manage it.

"Travis Foley hasn't done anything," she said, a bold-faced lie, cheeks flaming. "Blake, I'm fine. I promise you. There is absolutely nothing wrong with me."

"You're sure?"

"Of course I'm sure. It even stopped raining this morning. Finally!"

"What about the mine? Did you talk him into letting you back into the mine yet?"

"Actually," she said, looking at Travis, wanting to know it was okay with him, "we've come to an agreement."

Travis nodded. They were still in agreement.

"Really?" Blake sounded astonished. "How did you do that?"

She kept looking at Travis. "He said I was a brilliant

negotiator and that every argument I made, made perfect sense."

Laughter rumbled out of Travis, and he reached out and ticked the side of her breast.

She nearly slapped him away.

Blake fell into a thoroughly insulting silence.

"It's true," she told her brother.

"What did you have to give him?"

"I didn't give him anything." Okay, that was another bold-faced lie, but she thought she made the claim rather well. "What he really wants is for the McCords to leave him alone. I told him if I had a week or so to look for the diamond, and I couldn't find it, that's it. We're done. We won't bother him again. You have to promise me that, Blake. If I can't find it, we drop this."

"I don't get it. What's in it for him?"

"He genuinely loves it here," Paige said. "He likes the peace, the quiet, the privacy. I think you'd have to be a rancher to understand, but that means a lot to him. He hates having fortune hunters invading his space. Now, do we have a deal?"

Paige held the phone out between her and Travis. Her brother's voice came through loud and clear. "Yeah. You tell me the diamond's not there, we're done with the mine."

"With any of the old mines. With searching this ranch."

"Okay. Deal."

"Good. I'll call you as soon as the water goes down and we can get inside the mine."

"You be careful. If that man hurts you—"

She clicked the phone off and handed it back to Travis.

He gave her a long, studying look. "You think I don't trust you, Red? That I needed to hear him say it?"

"I wanted you to hear him say it. I wanted you to know you're doing the right thing by trusting me. I don't want you to have any doubts about that."

She watched him mull that over.

Maybe he had doubts and was fighting them.

Maybe he didn't.

She couldn't be sure, despite the thoroughly satisfying night she'd spent in his arms.

Chapter Eleven

Travis had been kept home by a conference call with his bankers, but he'd left her a present in the library before he headed out to work on his ranch.

Paige couldn't imagine what that might be.

She got up, wondering if Marta was already there. Normally at this time, she would be. Had Travis told her not to go to work in his room? Or maybe she'd gone into Paige's room and found a bed that hadn't been slept in.

Oh, well. Too late to worry about that now.

She put on the robe Travis left for her at the foot of the bed and padded across the hall through the family room and to the wing that held the other bedrooms. In her own room, she showered and dressed quickly, then headed for the library.

What could he have possibly given her?

On the desk in the library, she found a box. A big, old cardboard box.

"How romantic," she muttered to herself.

But inside…inside was an absolute treasure chest of information. All kinds of historical documents about the ranch, diaries of his ancestors and hers, maps, drawings, photos, everything.

She was so happy, she was practically bouncing with joy, couldn't wait to dig into it all.

Best of all, he had what looked like a complete record of the archaeologists' work in the mines with the petroglyphs last year!

She had their published report, but he had…everything!

She was so excited. This was…everything. Everything she needed. If anything could pinpoint the exact location of the diamond, it was the petroglyphs, and the archaeologists had mapped and photographed them all!

She was going to do it! She was going to find that diamond, and Blake would do what it took to save the family diamond empire, and then…

Paige thought of Travis.

And then what?

She pushed the thought out of her mind and settled into a chair with the archaeologists' material to start reading.

Travis caught hell from the ranch hands that day for not only starting the day obscenely late—and no explanations of conference calls with bankers were believed in the least—but also for being ridiculously happy.

Apparently, he'd been a bear to deal with for days.

He found he didn't care.

What he did care about was that there was a gorgeous redhead waiting back at the ranch for him, and he couldn't wait to get back to her, even if it was the first day in forever that it wasn't raining like crazy and there were a million things to be done around the ranch.

But he did his duty, as he always had, and got his work done, despite the temptations of *her.* Then he hurried with almost indecent speed back to the house once the work was done.

Cal offered to take care of Murph for him, and Travis actually agreed, which won him a long, hard look from Cal and a muttered, *Damn, she must be something,* under Cal's breath as Travis walked out of the barn.

For once, he wished a day's work didn't involve him coming home a mess, this time wet and muddy through and through.

He had just gotten his boots off in the mudroom and stood up to take off his shirt when she ran into the room, a beautiful smile on her face and launched herself into his arms, giving him no choice but to catch her.

"I'm filthy," he told her.

"I don't care," she claimed, as she laughed and kissed him.

"Okay, but what happened?" He'd never seen her this happy.

"You! My present! All those old records and the archaeologists' report!"

It was his turn to laugh. She was thrilled with a box of old records about the ranch?

"They're not exactly diamonds," he reminded her.

"No, they're better!" She kissed him again.

He gave her a skeptical look. Better than diamonds?

"You're talking to a geologist, remember? Trust me. They're better."

"Well, in that case…" He'd already gotten her filthy, wrapped around him the way she was, so now they both needed to get cleaned up. "Just how grateful are you, Red?"

She grinned. "You need someone to clean you up?"

He nodded.

"Allow me. Please."

"Only if I get to return the favor, Red."

She nodded. "Done."

They were lying in his bed, much later that night, Travis on his back, Paige curled against his side, him stroking that glorious red hair of hers, when he remembered the conversation he'd had with his father yesterday, about Charlie and Eleanor McCord.

Travis sighed, hating to bring their families into this room, this moment, but he knew she was worried about Charlie meeting the Foleys, and he didn't want to be keeping things from her.

He kept stroking her hair, his touch easy and soothing, he hoped, and said, "I meant to tell you, I talked to my father the other night, and I thought you'd like to know. He met Charlie."

She went to pull away from him, and he let her, only as far as to roll onto her back in the bed beside him, and he followed, up on his side, taking her face in his hand to turn it back toward him.

Because he was determined that they could talk about this and still be two people thoroughly enjoying each other in bed.

"When?" she whispered.

"I'm not sure. Just in the last few days."

She studied his face, obviously worried. "And?"

"And… they met. Listening to my father, it sounds like everybody's feelings are pretty much the same. All mixed up. Charlie is my father's son, except he's not, or he never has been. He doesn't know any of us, and none of us really knows what we feel yet. You should know, my father wanted to meet him all along, but decided to wait until Charlie was ready. Sounded like the whole thing was awkward, but civil. I'm sure they'll see each other again. My father said it's bound to take some time to get over the awkwardness and figure out where they go from here, but… He's a good man, Paige. A good father. And it meant something to him. It meant a lot. I could—"

He broke off.

"What?" she demanded. "Tell me."

"I think he actually started to cry while he was telling me about it," Travis admitted. "I don't remember my father ever shedding a tear over anything. He's a rock. He raised me and my two brothers all by himself after our mother died. The man's a force to be reckoned with, and this brought him to tears, just telling me about it. He'd never be cruel or even unkind to a child of his. You have to believe me about that."

"Okay. I do," she said. "And I'm glad that it meant so much to your father, and that you told me."

"I also told him I'd like to meet Charlie, whenever

Charlie's ready," Travis added. "That maybe he'd like to come to the ranch. Around here we put a man on a horse to see what he's made of."

That won him a smile.

"Red, tell me the kid can at least ride a horse respectably."

"He was born and raised in Texas. Of course, he can handle a horse."

"Good. I don't want to be embarrassed by the kid," he teased, leaning over and kissing her softly, then thinking, *damn,* he had to tell her the rest of it.

"What?" She seemed to have radar when it came to him holding back family news. "It's something bad. I knew it. You told me the good news. Now tell me the bad."

He groaned, closed his eyes and shook his head. "I don't know if it's bad, exactly—"

"If your reaction is any indication, it's bad. Travis, tell me—"

"My father said…he and your mother are…seeing each other."

She frowned. "Seeing… Like my mother is helping him to get to know Charlie?"

Travis shook his head. "No…seeing each other."

Paige looked incredulous. "Seeing as in…dating?"

"Worse," he admitted.

"They're sleeping together?" she cried, looking horrified.

"No! I mean…I don't know. I don't want to know. I didn't ask, and he didn't volunteer any information about that. He just…he said…he really cared about her all those years ago and that…he never stopped."

Paige scrambled to sit up in bed and keep the sheet covering her. Her mouth fell open, and she looked so shocked she couldn't even say anything.

"I know," he said. "I felt the same way when he told me. I just… That's what he said. That they've been apart all these years, and that they're seeing each other and they don't care what anyone in the family thinks about it anymore."

He waited, and she just sat there, looking like a million different questions were rushing through her head every moment, and he wished… He wished everything didn't have to be so damned complicated, with so many ways in which his family was entangled in hers.

"I meant to tell you last night, and we got… Well, you know what we did. But I don't want you to think I'm keeping secrets from you, either, and if you ask me what I think about this, I have no idea what to say. It's just…"

"Unreal," she said.

"Yes, it seems like it can't possibly be happening. But that's what he said. I take it this is not common knowledge in your family or mine, or we'd have heard about it by now from one of our siblings."

"Oh, I'd have heard about it. Blake, this morning, if he had any idea, would have told me all about it." She made a face, like a woman who dreaded what was to come.

"So I shouldn't have told you?" he asked.

She groaned. "I don't know. I don't think I want to know about the two of them. And I certainly don't want them to know about us. I just want to be here with you, without any of the family stuff between us. I know that's impossible, but…that's what I want."

"Well, how about…no more talk about the family while we're in bed?" he proposed, easing back down in the bed and tugging her down after him.

"Oh," she said, letting him pull her to him, those long legs of hers wrapping around his, her pretty breasts once more pressed against his chest. "That sounds like a great idea."

"Okay. Forget I said anything."

"I can do that," she promised. "Kiss me, and I'll forget right now."

He happily complied.

The days that followed, waiting for the floodwaters to recede, were idyllic, among the most joyous of her life, Paige decided.

She studied the historical records from the ranch by day and gave up her nights to Travis, gave herself, her body to him completely, while trying to tamp down any questions about risky emotional attachments, the future or messy family entanglements.

This was like a little present to herself, this time with him, and she meant to enjoy it to the fullest and try not to think about what happened later, once it was time for her to leave the ranch.

Except that she wanted Travis to always have the ranch.

The place had come alive to her after reading the old diaries of the women who'd lived and died here, the record of the struggles they faced, the men they'd loved, and all this life on the ranch had meant to them.

Travis loved it in that same way, and it should be his, she decided.

She wanted to be the one who made sure it was always his.

If she found the diamond, she thought she'd have the leverage to do that. She'd simply tell her family if they wanted her to give them the diamond, he got the ranch, period.

It was, as she'd told him, nothing more than stubborn pride and wanting to best the Foleys that would make anyone in her family hang on to the ranch anyway, and she was sick of the whole feud.

So that would be her parting gift to Travis.

His ranch.

And if, when this was over, he just let her go…she supposed she'd have to find the strength and the pride to go.

She wasn't going to think about it now.

She had a diamond to find.

And his records were going to help her. So far, she hadn't found any reference to the diamond at all, except for the same old speculation that it might be there. No one had put together the clue on the back of the old deed with the petroglyphs. No one said anything about ever searching in that way for the diamond.

So she thought it might still be here, even after all this time.

And with the archaeological records, she had the location of all the petroglyphs. The published report showed eight, but it turned out those were only the most clear, intact images the archaeologists had found. The complete records Travis had showed five more partial eagle images and their locations. With that, Paige had mapped out her own plan to search the mine, once the water went down.

Travis checked the mine every day and said it wouldn't be long now.

Which made her think, it was getting late. He'd be home soon.

She thought about what she might do that she hadn't already done with him, something he would enjoy coming home to....

Having her naked worked for him in a big way. So just waiting for him in his bed was always an option. Or walking into the shower with him, as he got cleaned up after a long day's work. That had proven to be very, very satisfying a few nights ago.

Maybe tonight, she really should wait until after dinner, because the man worked hard and he needed to keep up his strength. She could see that he was fed and then maybe take him into the library and take off her clothes and lie down on the rug in front of the fire.

Paige knew he'd like that. He'd wanted her there that first night, in the light of the fire, and she'd been too shy with him at first to really get into letting him watch while she slowly peeled off her clothes.

But she could do it now.

For him, she would.

She'd do anything for him.

He had that kind of sensual power over her.

It was scary and completely thrilling at the same time.

She'd never met a man like him, one who was so very much a man. A strong, kind, patient, gentle, outrageously sexy man who loved this land, this life with a kind of certainty she found so compelling. It made him seem so much more solid and trustworthy than any man she'd ever known.

Paige had met so many men who seemed to be just playing at life, moving along from this to that with no sense of commitment to anything.

Travis knew what he wanted. He worked hard every day to build the life he wanted, even knowing he might one day lose it to her family. He worked for it anyway.

And he seemed very happy to be sharing it with her. Whether that was simply sexual attraction or convenience…

Oh, please, don't let it be just that.

She didn't think she could stand it if, in the end, it was nothing but that.

Paige shook her head, refusing to think that way. She was here now. That was what mattered. They had this time together, and she intended to make the most of it.

Tonight, she was going to do something she'd never done for any man, because she hadn't ever wanted so much to please a man, to surprise him, to be a little daring, a little outrageous for him.

She was going to strip for Travis Foley.

She'd do it in front of the fire while he watched, if she didn't lose her nerve. Paige planned her wardrobe accordingly, looking for something with lots of buttons she could slowly undo and pretty, tiny, lace underwear. She'd even wear high heels for this. That's how crazy she was for the man.

He knew something was up when he walked in that night and saw her in those shoes.

"Are we going out?" he asked.

"Oh, no. We're staying in." She grinned wickedly.

"Okay," he said meekly. "Is there anything I should… do?"

"No, I'm going to take care of everything. You just do what you normally do. Go get cleaned up so I can feed you and then…you'll see."

"Yes, ma'am," he said, already headed for the shower.

"That was the sexiest thing I have ever seen in my life," he whispered into her ear later that evening as they lay on a blanket in front of the fire. "If it gets any better than that, I don't think my heart could take it."

He'd taken her in a frenzy of blazing heat and need and pleasure so deep and all encompassing, it was as if there was nothing left in the world, like what they shared erased everything else, consumed it.

As if they were the only two people in the world and nothing else even existed, much less mattered.

As if nothing had the power to come between them.

When she was in his arms like this, that's how she felt.

As if nothing could come between them.

Later, pleasantly tired and yet excited by all that she'd found out about the ranch, she wrapped herself up in an afghan, and he did, too, and she showed him some of her favorite old photos of the ranch, read him a few passages from old diaries with speculation about the diamond, and then showed him the deed itself and what she and Blake had found.

There was a scanned copy of it in her e-mail box. She'd had Blake send it to her earlier.

She brought it up on the computer and showed him the image.

"See, right here?" She pointed to the border of the deed, made with hundreds of tiny eagles.

"That's the same image used to mark the Eagle Mine," he said, leaning over her shoulder as she sat at his desk.

"Yes. And look here, this corner. It's hard to see on the scan—and even on the actual map, you have to really be looking to see it—but this one eagle, in his talon is a diamond."

He leaned closer to the computer screen, then shook his head. "I don't see it."

"Well, it's there. I think it's telling us not just that the diamond was hidden in the Eagle Mine, but that the image of the eagle marks the spot where the diamond was buried. The image used on the petroglyphs is the same as the one on the deed, as the eagle holding the diamond in his claw. I know where all those images are because you gave me the archaeologists' report, along with the maps they made. Travis, we can find it! We're going to find that diamond!"

He turned and sat on the edge of the desk, shaking his head.

"You thought I was crazy, didn't you?"

"Maybe. A little."

"But see? It's all here. It all makes sense. The diamond has to be at one of these spots, and there are only thirteen of them. We're going to find it."

"Okay, but can we find it tomorrow? Or two days from now? Or next week?" he asked, trailing kisses from her bare shoulder up to her neck.

She laughed, shivering because it felt so good, and

went to close the image and the e-mail it came in, only then noticing she had six different e-mails from Gabby, all within a two-hour span.

"My cousin Gabby's going nuts about something," she said. "She probably found out my mother's dating your father."

"Uh-huh," he said, teasing her ear with his tongue. "Tomorrow. They'll all be just as crazy tomorrow."

He was right. They would. But just as she was closing the program, she noticed the last subject heading.

Penny in trouble.

A shiver worked its way through her body, this one not of pleasure but of uneasiness, of dread.

"Travis, wait," she said, pulling away from him. "Something's wrong with my sister."

He lifted his head and looked at the screen.

Paige opened the e-mail, scared of what she was going to find.

Gabby wrote:

Wanted to be able to tell you this on the phone, but you never answer your phone. Where are you? Penny's been seeing someone in secret for months now, and I'm terrified for her.

Paige, it's Jason Foley!

She finally admitted that she's in love with Jason Foley, and I can't believe this is all a coincidence. That there's all this stuff going on with the search for the diamond, and Jason Foley just happens to show up and seduce one of the McCords.

Tried to tell Penny, but she wouldn't listen to me.

You have to call her. You have to warn her, before he breaks her heart.

—Gabby

Paige froze.

I can't believe this is all a coincidence.

Jason Foley seducing Penny, at the same time Paige just happens to find herself here with Travis, thinking herself in love with him.

Beside her, reading over her shoulder, Travis backed away and swore long and loud.

One look at his face told her everything she needed to know.

"Both of us?" she asked, clutching the afghan closer to her naked body.

She was sitting here, naked in his library, having just performed a striptease for him, then had sex with him on the rug in front of the fire, crazy to please him.

And he and his brother had...

What?

"Was it some sort of bet?" She threw the words at him. "Which one of you could bed one of the McCord twins first?"

"No!" He looked outraged that she'd even think it.

"And did you win? Or did he?"

"It wasn't a bet! I'm not like that! How can you think I'm like that?"

"Well, there's no way this is a coincidence. Your brother seducing my sister, and you seducing me—"

"I didn't know you were coming here. How could I

possibly know you were going to show up on this ranch—"

"You knew we were looking for the diamond—"

"My brothers thought your family was up to something, but they always think that. They care so much more about this stupid feud than I do. I just want to be here and run this ranch. That's all I want. You know that. I told you that. You've been here. You've seen for yourself how much I love this ranch. Haven't you?"

Paige started to cry then, so mad at herself for giving into that need, so mad that he had to see it. "I saw your face just a minute ago, before you could hide it. You knew what your brother was doing—"

"I never agreed to do anything to you, not hurting you or using you or seducing you. I didn't want anything to do with my family's obsession with your family or that stupid diamond."

"So you're trying to tell me, your brother just happened to seduce my sister at the same time you seduced me—"

"Hey, I don't remember there being a great deal of seduction involved. I remember two people who just flat-out wanted each other and couldn't keep their hands off each other. And I'll remind you, I'm the one who stopped that first night. Not you. I could have done anything I wanted with you that night, and you know it. But I didn't."

Paige felt like all the blood rushed out of her head at that, ashamed and embarrassed and getting even madder.

Just how good was he at this game?

"You need to remember, too," he went on, "that you climbed into my bed knowing exactly who I was, wanting me despite everything that was going on with the diamond and the family feud. You wanted me anyway, just the way I wanted you."

She closed her eyes, hating herself and what she'd done, what she'd let him do to her.

"You and your brother had a plan," she said, glaring at him.

"No, we didn't—"

"I saw your face, Travis! When you first read that e-mail, you knew. I saw the guilt on your face—"

"Over what my brother had done to your sister!" he yelled. "I know you love her, and I knew... I knew—"

Paige gasped. "You knew what he was going to do? He deliberately set out to get close to her? To seduce her? And you knew all along?"

Travis closed his eyes and turned away, swearing under his breath as he did.

Obviously, he'd known.

And that thing she felt deep inside, that was her heart, breaking in two.

She pulled the afghan tighter against her, feeling more naked and humiliated than she'd ever been in her life. Getting to her feet, she tried to shove him out of her way. But he got hold of her and didn't let go, grabbing her by the arms and pulling her close, making her look at him.

Making her let him see just how much he'd hurt her? Why did he have to see that, too? Hadn't he done enough already?

"Listen to me. You've been here with me all this time. You know me. Don't you?"

"I know you knew something about your brother seducing my sister—"

"Okay, yes, I knew. I'm sorry. I didn't even remember what he was going to try to do until right now. But when I saw your cousin's e-mail…. Yes, I knew."

Paige felt like her whole body started to shake at once, like there was no solid ground anywhere, nothing to catch her if she just sank to the floor.

He knew!

"Look, Paige, I got a call from my brothers months ago. They were sure your family was up to something to do with the diamond. They wanted to make all sorts of plans, and I told you already, I didn't want anything to do with the whole mess. I just want to run my ranch and have everybody leave me the hell alone. So it wasn't like I was in on planning this. I was only half listening to them at this point. I do that. My eyes glaze over, and I start thinking about cattle prices or fences that need to be replaced, things like that when they start talking family feud with me. But yes, when I saw your cousin's e-mail, I remembered Jason saying something months ago about needing to get information on what your family was up to, and thinking he could get it from Penny."

"She doesn't know anything!" Paige cried. "She's not like me. She's sweet and innocent. I don't think she's ever even slept with a man before in her life, and now she thinks she's in love with him, Travis. How could he do that to her? How can you play with people's hearts that way?"

He pulled her close, tucked her head against his shoulder and held her while she cried, and she let him.

Dammit, she just let him.

"I'm sorry," he said, again and again. "I'm so sorry. All I agreed to do was watch out for trespassers at the old mines. That's it. I swear to you. And then...there you were."

"I came right to you," she whispered. "I made it so easy for you."

"No," he swore. "It wasn't like that. You know it wasn't."

She pulled away from him, staring him in the face. "Then what was it, exactly? A lucky coincidence?"

"No, it was damned inconvenient. It still is, and you know it. You made me want you despite who you are and how complicated this is, and you want me despite all of that, too."

She wanted to believe him.

Oh, she did.

He was such a dangerous man, because even now, she wanted to believe him.

"These last few days, I haven't been thinking of anything but you," he said.

God, she wanted to believe him.

"Of hurrying back here every night so I can be with you. It's like the whole world is just gone, and I love the rain and even the stupid flood, because it's keeping everybody else away, and it's just you and me. That's all I want. Just you and me."

She gave him a hard look, probably spoiled completely by the tears in her eyes.

"I have to go call my sister," she said with as much outrage and indignation as she could muster against him. "I have to go tell her that the man she thinks she's in love with has been lying to her all along, just to get information about our family."

He took that like a slap in the face, backing away, hands up and off of her, breathing hard, his jaw as hard as granite.

"Fine," he said. "Believe what you want. Make the call."

Chapter Twelve

She cried some more in her room before she could get herself together enough to call her sister, dreading how much what she had to say was going to hurt Penny, whom Paige had always tried to protect from the big, bad world.

Her sweet, dreamy, artsy sister, delicate as a fairy and always seeing men through a kind of filmy, romantic haze.

She hated Travis's brother for this, absolutely hated him.

But she wasn't going to think of Travis himself or anything he'd done to her or how she felt about it. It was too new, too raw. It hurt too much, and she just didn't know what to believe.

Finally, her tears stopped enough that she thought she could do it, she could tell her sister this awful thing. She picked up the phone by her bed, and Penny came on the line, sounding so happy Paige nearly started to cry again.

"Oh, my God! What is it? What's wrong?" Penny cried.

"Nothing. I just… I have to tell you something, and—"

"I have to tell you something, too, but mine is good and it can wait. You go first. What's wrong?"

Oh, this was awful!

Jason Foley should be strung up by his ankles and left to fry in the hot Texas sun. Paige would find the rope and help do it herself, and her brothers would help her.

"Paige, you're scaring me," her sister said.

"I know. I'm sorry. Penny, I'm so sorry about this. I love you. You know that, right? And I'll help you get through this. I promise."

"Get through what?"

"Jason Foley," Paige said.

Silence came from the other end.

"You've been seeing Jason Foley, right?"

"Yes," her sister said. "And I know that no one's going to like that, that no one's going to understand, and I'm so sorry I couldn't bring myself to tell you sooner. It was awful, trying to keep a secret like this from you. I just… All the feelings I have are all so overwhelming, so new that I can still hardly believe it myself, but he's not who you think he is, Paige, I swear. He's not the man any of us think he is. He's wonderful, and sweet and kind, and I'm in love with him. I think he's in love with me, too—"

"He's using you to get information about our family." Paige just blurted it out.

Penny laughed. "No, he's not."

"Yes, he is."

Penny hesitated. "He wouldn't do that. He's not like that."

"Yes, he is. Penny, honey, I'm at the ranch right now. I'm at Travis Foley's ranch, looking for the diamond. Travis was with me when I read Gabby's e-mail telling me you were seeing Jason, and Travis knew…. He knew what his brother was going to do. Jason planned this months ago to try to find out what we were doing to find the diamond."

"No. That's crazy! You're at Travis Foley's ranch?"

"Yes. Honey, listen to me. I'm sorry, but Travis admitted the whole thing. The Foleys were convinced our family was up to something. Jason thought he could get the information from you. By getting to know you, by pretending he was interested in you."

Again, silence.

"I'm so sorry. I could just kill them both with my bare hands, I swear. I will make them pay," Paige promised. "We'll all make them pay for what Jason did to you."

"I thought… I thought I was in love with him."

"I know. Gabby told me. I'm so sorry, honey."

"Paige, I slept with him," she confessed.

Yes, they were going to kill him. String him up and let the ants slowly kill him or maybe buzzards. Texas was full of buzzards.

Jason Foley deserved it all.

"It's…" Penny started laughing, a sad, scary sound. "It's even worse than that, I'm afraid."

Worse?

What could be worse than that?

"Because, I just figured out that… Well, I'm pregnant," Penny confessed. "I'm going to have Jason Foley's baby."

It was a horrible night.

Paige cried. She paced the floor, scrubbed her skin clean in the shower, trying to erase every touch of Travis Foley from her body. She burned with shame the way she'd fallen all over him, practically begging him to take her that first night and then even trying to get all the so-called family business out of the way so they could be together, despite everything else.

And the way she'd given herself to him….

Completely, without reservation, nothing held back.

Not even her heart.

She'd stripped for him in his library and had sex with him on the rug in front of his fireplace, like a woman just crazy-mad for him.

And he…

She had no idea what he felt for her or what she could trust that he'd ever said.

Could a man really just forget that his brother was going to seduce her sister to get information out of her? Was that something anyone could really forget?

Although, she had to admit, her family said a lot of things about his, and there were times when she got sick of the whole thing, too, when she tried her best to tune it all out.

She wanted to believe Travis. And as he'd pointed out, he hadn't seduced her, unless he was even better at it than she imagined and she was just much more gullible and hadn't even realized what he was doing. Because it seemed to her, it was completely mutual, as he claimed.

She buried her face in her pillow and cried herself to sleep.

When she woke the next morning, the sun was high in the sky.

It was nearly eleven.

Her head hurt, and her eyes felt like they'd been rubbed with sandpaper. Her throat ached from crying, and she felt the need to scrub her skin some more, to try to forget every sweet, sexy touch of his body against hers.

She'd have just stayed in bed all day, if it weren't for the fact that her sister was heartbroken and pregnant, and she still had a diamond to find and a family about to go broke if she didn't.

Thank goodness she hadn't told Travis Foley that, at least.

He hadn't had to seduce her to get information out of her. She'd just given it all to him, she realized in horror.

She'd told him exactly where the diamond was!

He could have found it already! He could kick her off this ranch today and take the maps from the archaeology dig and find the diamond himself! He could hold her prisoner here, to keep her quiet and isolated from her family, while he found the diamond!

Paige scrambled up and into her clothes, rushing into the hallway and through the house.

Marta looked at her as if she was nuts when she tried all the doors and found them open, no one trying to stop her from going anywhere.

Of course, she couldn't get off this ranch without Travis. Or at least, without one of his horses or his trucks.

Next, she tried the phones.

All working.

She could call for help right now, if she wanted to. Warn her brother about everything and have him send an army to guard the opening of the mine and the diamond inside.

Paige started to dial and then Travis walked in, looking wary and bone tired and not sure what kind of reception he'd get from her today.

"You need to make a call?" he asked. "I can go into the kitchen, if you want some privacy."

She wasn't sure whether to believe him. "You'll let me make a call?"

He frowned. "Why wouldn't I?"

"Because I could tell my brother what you did and what your brother did, and that I told you exactly where the diamond is."

"I assumed you already had," he said, looking resigned to it all being public knowledge by now.

So, she could just tell her family everything and he'd let her?

Paige thought of her mother then, for the first time. Her mother who was supposedly dating Rex Foley now.

Oh, God!

Her mother!

"Tell me your father seeing my mother has nothing to do with any of this? That at least that part is real."

His jaw went tight with anger. "My father claims he's been crazy about your mother since long before she even met *your* father, and that his feelings haven't changed all these years. You believe that if you want to. I can't stop you if you don't."

Paige wasn't sure. She just couldn't be sure of anything.

And Charlie... What was this all going to do to Charlie and any relationship he might have with the Foleys now?

She didn't know about that, either, and so she decided to try to deal with the situation at hand. Her and Travis, the ranch and the diamond.

"Are you going to keep me here?" she asked him.

"Keep you here? I haven't been keeping you here, Paige. There's a flood that's been keeping you here."

"So you'd just let me leave?" she tried.

"Tell me where you want to go. We'll do our best to get you there."

"Off this ranch?"

"Paige, what the devil are you talking about?" he snapped.

She took a breath, felt like crying again. "I don't know. I thought...you know where the diamond is. I told you. I told you how to find it. I thought—"

"That I'd hold you prisoner here, and go get the diamond for myself and my family?"

He was so loud, so angry, she nearly took a step back from the sheer force of his words.

It sounded crazy when he said it like that, and yet...this whole thing between them had been just crazy.

"It's worth a fortune," she said.

"I already have what most people would consider a fortune. My family struck it rich in oil. I suspect you've heard about it. There's nothing I really want that I can get from that diamond," he said bitterly.

And she wondered exactly what it was Travis Foley might want.

Not her.

Surely not her.

He couldn't have meant that. He was furious with her and probably cursed her whole family right now.

But why was he furious? It was his brother who seduced her sister for information, while Travis... She wasn't sure what Travis had done, exactly, or why he'd done it.

He certainly was the picture of an outraged man, and that just didn't fit.

"So," she began. "The diamond..."

"I assume you still want to find it? And then get the hell off my ranch?"

She nodded.

"That's what I came to tell you. The water's gone down. We can get into the mine today, if you want."

Just like that?

Their previous deal stood?

"You're still going to honor our agreement?"

"Why wouldn't I? Nothing to do with our agreement has changed. Your family's determined to have that diamond, and as long as you believe it's here, one of the McCords is going to be here, bothering me, trying to get it. As I see it, the easiest way to get rid of you all seems to be to let you look your fill, until you either give up or find the damned thing. So go look, please, and let's get this over with. And then you can go."

* * *

Travis took her that afternoon to the mine, insisting that he be the one to watch over her while she looked. He didn't trust anyone but himself to make sure she was safe, and he was at least going to make sure she didn't get hurt on this stupid family quest of hers.

That her family would send a woman, a young, beautiful woman to do something like this still made him a little bit crazy. He didn't care that she was the geologist of the family.

It wasn't the kind of job he thought a man should send a woman to do.

Of course, he came from a family that sent his brother to seduce her sister for information, so it seemed he didn't have much room to talk in the what-your-family-would-do area.

He was still furious with the lot of them.

For the whole, crazy feud.

For the lost diamond.

For her sister getting hurt the way she no doubt had been hurt when she heard the news about Jason.

For Charlie, the brother he never knew about until a few months ago, and the father who'd just admitted to always being in love with a woman other than Travis's mother.

For all of it.

And for the woman who'd shown up on his ranch, him not knowing who she was, for the way she'd bewitched him with need and wanting. For the way he'd do just about anything for her, and she didn't even believe it or care.

For the whole damned mess.

But she just had to find that diamond, so he stood there, watching over her and waiting for her, to make sure she didn't get herself killed over the stupid thing. All so he could stand by and watch her walk away from him when her search was over.

It was all so stupid. And completely infuriating. How was he ever going to let her go? How could he ever convince her to stay?

She finally gave up her search shortly before sunset, coming out of the mine cold and grubby and looking completely worn-out. She'd cried herself to sleep the night before. He'd stood on the other side of her bedroom wall, listening to her, fighting the urge to go to her and beg her to believe him about what he'd known and what he'd done, to beg her to forgive him.

So she had to be exhausted now. But she was still beautiful and he still wanted her, dammit.

"We can come back tomorrow?" she asked.

He nodded.

Fine.

They'd come back tomorrow, and they'd make this thing between them about nothing but the stupid diamond now.

Chapter Thirteen

In the end, Paige didn't tell anyone else in her family anything about Jason Foley or what he'd done.

It was Penny's secret to tell, she decided.

Penny was the one who'd been hurt the most by it, and she had a baby to think about, too.

She called Penny the night after spending a second day searching the mine with no luck, Travis just letting her look, standing so somberly by, not trying to talk her into or out of anything. Just letting her do what she had to do.

Paige didn't understand him any better than she understood herself or her feelings for him, so she mostly tried not to think about any of it.

She had a job to do, and she'd do it.

Part of that was taking care of her poor sister.

It took four tries before her sister would even

answer the phone and when she did, before Paige could even say anything else, Penny just blurted out, "Just don't ask me what I'm going to do, okay? Because I don't know yet."

"Okay," Paige agreed.

"I'm sorry. I just…I don't know."

"That's fine, honey. I know it's all a shock. I just…I wanted to be sure I understand where you are in this. Are you sure you're pregnant?"

"I…well, it looks like it. I'm late, and I took one of those home pregnancy tests. Three, actually. All positive."

"Okay, but you haven't seen a doctor yet?" Paige tried.

"No. Not yet."

"Well, don't you think you should? I mean… Surely sometimes those home tests are wrong—" They could hope.

"Three times in a row?" Penny reminded her.

"Okay, probably not three times in a row. But still, you want to have a doctor check you out, make sure you're healthy and that the baby's okay."

"I guess so," Penny admitted.

"Let me give you my gynecologist's name. She's great. Very gentle, and she'll be completely supportive. I promise." Paige gave her the name, then as gently as she could told her, "I haven't said anything to anyone about this. I'm not going to. It's up to you. If you want me to tell them or be with you when you tell anyone, I will. I'll do whatever you want, whatever I can to help."

"Thank you." Her sister started to cry softly.

"And you didn't ask me, and I probably shouldn't say this, but I think as soon as you've seen the doctor, you should go see that rat Jason Foley and tell him exactly how well his little seduction plan worked—"

"Paige, please—"

"He should know what he did."

"It wasn't just him," she cried. "It was me, too. I wanted him so much."

"And I'm sure he knew just how to make you want him. There's no telling how many women he's seduced over the years, the rat!"

"I can't tell him," she argued. "Not now. It's all too new, too crazy, and I have no idea what I'm going to do about this. No, I can't tell him. You promise you won't tell him, either. That you won't tell anyone."

Oooh, that was a tough promise to make.

True, she'd just promised a moment ago to not do anything her sister didn't want her to do, but she'd never imagined part of that would be letting Jason Foley off the hook completely.

"Paige, promise me. Right now."

"Okay," she said reluctantly. "But you have to tell him eventually."

"Mom kept Charlie's secret for twenty-one years. Do you think we're all better off for knowing?"

"I don't know," Paige admitted.

"Neither do I, so I'm not telling Jason anything right now."

By the end of the fifth day of searching, with no sign of the diamond, Paige was exhausted, frustrated and very, very sad.

Travis had been stonily silent, icily polite, doing what

she needed from him to help with the search but nothing else. Blake sounded more defeated each day when she talked to him and poor Penny still had no idea what she was going to do about Jason Foley or her baby.

How had everything gone so wrong?

Paige sat on the ground just outside the mine entrance, cold, wet, dirty, having no idea what to do next.

She'd never really given up on anything before.

Travis stood just beyond the rock overhang outside the mine, waiting, finally saying, "That was it? The last of the eagle markings? You checked the last ones today?"

She nodded. "Every one mapped by the archaeology team you let explore the mine last year. Unless they missed one or didn't record the location of one—"

"They went over every inch of that place. I thought they were crazy, how excited they were to get inside that mine and then to see how carefully they checked the walls. I went down with them a couple of times to see what all the fuss was about. I have trouble thinking they missed anything."

Paige shook her head. "I knew it was a long shot. I just didn't want to admit it to my brother. I mean, even if Elwin Foley came to the ranch after surviving the ship-wreck and hid the diamond in the Eagle Mine, it's been so long. My ancestors worked the mine, bringing out the silver for years. How they could have done that and never found the diamond... I don't know. I hoped it was possible, but... How could they have missed buried treasure when they were mining here all those years?"

"I don't see how they could have," Travis agreed. "And...I'm not trying to be insensitive or to start a fight here, but Paige, why are you letting your family put this on you? This pressure to find the diamond? I mean, it's not like your family needs the money. Can't you just let it go? Tell them to back off? Or to find the damned thing themselves, if it's so important to them?"

Which sounded curiously like he was trying to take care of her. Which was the last thing she'd have expected from him.

And then she was just sick of the whole mess and all the misery it had brought her, all that she felt or thought she'd felt for Travis Foley and how much she missed him, even when he was right here beside her. She couldn't even let herself think of how she dreaded leaving the ranch and never seeing him again, even if she didn't really trust him and was furious at his family.

It was all just such a mess.

She didn't care anymore, so she just told him everything.

"The thing is, we do really need the money," she confessed. "My father…he wasn't the greatest guy in the world, and I guess that didn't just extend toward personal relationships. He wasn't much of a businessman, either. My brother Blake is much better at it, but I guess when he took over the business after our father died, it was in trouble. Serious trouble. Blake's doing everything he can, but I really think it's going to take a miracle to save the family business now, and we were banking on that miracle being the diamond. So, yes, it matters. It matters that much."

She looked at him, knowing she'd told him much more than she needed to, things his family would just love to hear about the McCords. But what did it matter now?

If business was that bad, it wouldn't be a secret much longer.

She couldn't imagine her family without the jewelry stores, without that work to do. It had been much more than a source of income. It had been what they all did together, Blake managing the business, her overseeing the buying of raw stones worldwide and cutting many of them herself, her sister designing settings for the stones, her cousin Gabby the international face and spokeswoman for the stores. It held them altogether, gave them a common goal and a strong sense of pride.

What would they do now?

"I just feel like I let my whole family down," she said.

"Hey, it's not your fault if the diamond isn't there," Travis began.

"I know, but...I just really thought I could find it. Once Blake showed me the deed with that diamond in the eagle's talon, I was so sure. But we've searched every eagle marking in this mine, and it's just not there. Every one—"

But then as she said it, she realized she was wrong.

Oh, they'd searched every one inside the mine.

But right at that moment, she was looking at one spot they hadn't searched.

"Paige?" Travis asked.

She walked over to the big, heavy stone that stood just outside the mine, marking it as the Eagle Mine with an eagle carved into the stone.

"We didn't search here," she said, the idea bouncing

around in her head at warp speed. "It's the same eagle, the same image from the deed. And it's not in the mine! They wouldn't have disturbed this area as they mined for silver, so that's how Elwin could have hidden it at the mine, without worrying about anyone finding it accidentally as they mined the silver! Travis! I think this is it!"

She turned back to him, and he looked skeptical, like she was grasping at straws or just could not admit defeat. But she didn't think so.

This hiding place... This made sense. The diamond would likely be safe here, even if the mine was opened to get the silver out.

She ran over to the rock, tried to move it and found that it wouldn't even budge.

Turning back to Travis, she pleaded with him. "Please? This one last place? If it's not here, I'm done. Promise."

"All right. But quit trying to move that rock. You'll never manage." He pulled a rope off of his saddle. "If we're lucky, Murph can move it."

He looped the rope around the rock, then tied the other end to the saddle horn, and took his place by the horse's head. "Come on, boy. Show us how strong you are."

The horse started backing up, until the line stretched taut and then Murph dug in with his big hind legs and very, very slowly eased back some more until the rock tipped over.

Travis undid the rope, and Paige grabbed a shovel and started digging. A moment later, Travis grabbed another small shovel and started helping her.

They were three feet down when she hit something.

Her heart started racing.

Carefully, they cleared dirt from the top, finding a rectangular-shaped object.

"Tell me it's not a rock," she begged.

"If it is, it's the most perfectly shaped rectangular rock I've ever found," Travis said. "And we won't get it out this way. Start digging on the left side. We need room on at least two sides to pry it loose."

They dug some more.

Finally, Travis could get his hands on two sides of the thing and ease it forward and to the left enough to dislodge it and then lift it to the surface.

Paige gasped.

When the dirt was brushed away, she saw that it was a treasure chest!

An ancient-looking silver chest, if Paige wasn't mistaken, encrusted with precious stones, emeralds, rubies, maybe even diamonds.

"Go ahead," Travis said. "Open it. You've earned the right."

Her hands shook, literally, she was so excited.

The lid came open with a creaking sound and on top was an old, dirty cloth.

She pulled the cloth away and gasped once more.

Coins.

Old silver coins.

Hundreds of them.

"The ship supposedly held a fortune in old Spanish silver," she told him.

She dipped her hands inside the coins, digging in one side of the chest and then the other, finally coming up with a cloth, the ends tied together around something big and heavy.

All the breath went out of her, as she sat the cloth down on top of the coins and just looked at it.

Travis laughed and pulled out his pocketknife, cutting the string that held the cloth together.

"Go ahead. Look," he told her.

"It's huge. I mean, I knew the diamond was supposed to be huge, as big as the Hope Diamond, and I've seen the Hope Diamond before. It was huge, too, but I just don't know if this—"

"Red, just look and see," he said, still sounding amused.

She closed her eyes, took a breath, then opened her eyes and pulled the cloth away.

There inside the old, disintegrating cloth was a stone roughly the size of an egg, primitively cut but glowing yellow and startling in its clarity.

She held it up to the light of the setting sun, watching the stone come to life with light, shimmering all over the different facets of the perfect, flawless stone.

"That's it," she told Travis. "It's the Santa Magdalena Diamond! We found it!"

And then she threw her arms around him, let him pick her up and whirl her around while she laughed like she never had before and cried, and then, when he finally set her back on her feet, kissed him like she'd never let him go.

Paige had to be dreaming.

She had the diamond in her backpack on the way back to the ranch house, and for a moment back there,

Travis had kissed her like a man who never wanted to let her go.

Could he really not want to let her go?

Because it was breaking her heart to think of leaving him. They'd kept things from each other, and hurt each other, and their families had hated each other for years, but he was still the best man she'd ever met. The sexiest, the sweetest, the kindest, the most protective, the most gentle man.

She didn't care if his last name was Foley.

It was hard to accept what his brother had done to her sister, and that was likely to be a sore spot between them for years, not just for the two of them, but for both their families. And there was still all that stuff with their parents dating and Charlie trying to find his own way amidst both families.

Could they ever put all that behind them? Or put it all aside somehow and just be two people who were crazy about each other?

The last few days had been the worst of her life, thinking he'd lied to her and that his whole family was out to hurt hers and that one day soon, she'd be leaving this ranch and never come back.

So it was time to put her heart on the line, to take a leap of faith.

They got back to the ranch near sunset, and he had Cal take care of both their horses. He carried the treasure chest, wrapped in a blanket, into his house, and she had the diamond.

"Why don't you go get cleaned up, Red, and then we'll try to sort this thing out," Travis said.

She was a mess. It seemed the whole time she'd known him, she'd been either dirty or wet or both.

It had been the strangest kind of courtship.

Nerves eating away at her, she ran through the shower, dressed quickly and came to find him in the library, the treasure chest and the diamond on the table in front of the big, leather sofa.

Paige closed her eyes and prayed for strength and a little bit of pride and hopefully some poise, because she had the oddest feeling that the rest of her life depended on the outcome of this conversation, and at the moment, she was scared to say a word.

How did people do this? Get their hearts broken and survive? Because she'd been hurt before, but she'd never cared like this, never risked so much, never been so scared.

"I guess we have a few more things to negotiate, Red," he said, looking so big and strong and gorgeous she could have wept right then and there.

"Negotiate?" They were going to talk business? Now?

Had he forgotten that kiss at the mine after they'd found the diamond? Had it meant nothing to him?

She tried not to let her hurt feelings show. "Okay."

"I guess we're back to your family versus mine," he said.

Oh, God. That was it? She very nearly did cry then.

"I take it you want the diamond, free and clear, no claim of ownership from my family?" he asked.

"Not...ownership, exactly, but no fight. I'd really like to do this without a fight, Travis. Especially not a long battle in court over who owns what. I don't think any of us would benefit from that."

"Okay. I'm not dying for a long, drawn-out fight," he admitted.

"I was hoping we could come to some agreement… you and me…that we could get both our families to agree to."

"So, what do you want?" he asked.

As if it were that easy….

She unwrapped the diamond, picked it up and held it in her open hand, letting it sparkle and shine for him.

"This is… Well, there simply isn't another stone like this in the world. Not of this size and color and clarity. It's a national treasure. International, actually, and, as I see it, the only rightful place for it is in a museum. The Smithsonian in Washington D.C., I would think, where the Hope Diamond is. They were supposed to be a pair, thousands of years ago. It only seems right that they're together again."

He frowned. "That's it? All this fuss over finding it, and all you want is for my family to let yours donate it to a museum?"

"Actually, I was thinking we could do it jointly, my family and yours. Claim joint ownership of it. No fight. You and I found it—"

"You found it, Red. I was just along for the ride to make sure you didn't get hurt going after that thing."

"No." She shook her head. "We found it together, on land that both our families have a claim to, in a mine that both our families can claim, too. But I don't want us to fight anymore. I'm sick of the whole fight, and this… Well, to me, it's simple. The diamond belongs in a museum, where millions of people can see it, and it would be a huge tax write-off for both our families, I'm sure. So it's not without benefit to your family…."

He laughed incredulously. "A tax write-off? That's what you're offering my family?"

"And a chance to do the right thing with the diamond. I mean, you don't want to just keep it? Do you?"

"No, Red. I don't want to keep it. But I thought your family needed it desperately. I thought that's what this was all about? Saving your family?"

"We just need it for a little while. Maybe six months? To display in the jewelry stores. And then, we'll give it to the museum," she tried.

"That's it? Display the diamond for six months, and your family's business is saved?"

He said it like he might actually care and not want her family's business to go under. She took a bit of hope in that.

"Well, no. We're hoping to corner the market on canary diamonds. My brother has everything in place, just waiting for us to find the diamond. It's the publicity from finding the Santa Magdalena, and… You're not going to like this part, Travis. You're probably going to have a lot of people wanting to get onto this ranch, at least for a while, to cover the story and see exactly where we found it and the old mine. I'm sorry, but—"

"Thank God," he said, sounding thoroughly relieved.

"What?"

She didn't get it.

He'd hate having all those people invade his ranch.

"I was counting on having something you wanted really badly, Red. Something to negotiate with, to get what I want," he said, grinning that beautiful grin of his at her.

"What? I don't understand."

"That's the way it works, right? If I have something you want, badly, then you have to give me something I want in return. I'm counting on that."

She stared at him, thinking she was missing something here. Really missing something.

"It's a negotiation, Red," he said, looking so gorgeous, reminding her of him standing in a tuxedo at some party, looking like a man who owned the world, who knew just what he wanted and knew he was going to get it. "Ask me what I want."

And then she started to shake, she was so scared.

What did he want?

"You want the ranch. I know that. I told you I'd do everything I could to get my mother—"

"Aw, baby." He knelt down in front of her as she sat there, trembling and practically unable to speak, took her face in his hand and kissed her softly, sweetly. "Ask me what I want even more than that."

"More than that?" she whispered.

"I want you. And I'll tell you right now, I'm not giving an inch here. No wiggle room. You can have the stupid diamond. You can do anything you want with it. My whole family can have a fit. I don't care. But I get you."

Tears filled her eyes, and spilled over, running down her cheeks. "So…what do you intend to do with me?"

"Keep you. Make you mine. Forever. That's my plan. I should warn you, too, that I don't have a diamond right this minute, and I bet a man who shows up to propose to a woman whose family owns a jewelry empire had better have a really nice diamond. Probably one from her family's stores. So I can't do this properly right this minute, but I can't wait, either. Paige McCord, say you'll marry me."

She nodded, sheer joy spilling over inside of her, as the tears ran down her cheek.

"Say you'll forgive me for everything my family has done to yours over the years," he asked. "I'll forget everything yours has done to mine, and we'll both promise to never let our families' problems with each other come between us. And marry me. I need you to say it, Red. I love you, and I need to hear you say it."

"Yes," she said. "I will. I love you, too. I've never loved any man the way I love you. And I don't care what anyone in either of our families has to say about it. I just don't care."

He got very serious for a moment. "One thing. You have to be honest with me about this. You could be happy? Living here at the ranch?"

She nodded. "I might have to take off a couple of times a year, for the stores. I buy most of the uncut stones we sell in the stores."

"As long as you come back," he said.

"And I like to cut the stones we sell myself. I could… Maybe I could have an office here at the ranch?"

"Anything you need, Red. Anything," he promised.

She smiled so big it was hard to talk. "I love this ranch. I think it's beautiful here."

"And you could spend your life here? Be happy here?"

"As long as you're here with me," she said.

"Well, then. I think we've got ourselves a deal, Red."

* * *

He pulled her into his arms, and it wasn't long before she was naked on that rug in front of his fireplace once again, thoroughly content.

Life was so good, she thought, snuggling beside him, wrapped in an afghan and warmed by the fire. It was unbelievably, amazingly good.

He sighed heavily, let his hands move through her hair. "You know, it's almost Thanksgiving. I think we need to have a big family dinner, right here at the ranch. Your family and mine."

"Oh, Travis. Do you think they're ready for that? For all of us to be in the same room together?"

"I think they're just going to have to get used to it. Because you and I are already together, and our parents might be someday, and there's already Charlie…. I mean, because of him, we're all already family. It's time we started acting like one. I say, we invite my family and yours to Thanksgiving dinner."

"Okay, if you're sure." She wasn't looking forward to sharing him with anyone just yet, but supposed it had to happen sooner or later.

"I'll tell them that you and I are getting married, and that's that. We're not going to ask for permission, because no one's talking us out of it, no matter what. And you can tell them that you and I found the diamond, and that we've decided to donate it in both our families' names to the Smithsonian."

She could handle that. "No arguments. No discussion. Done deal?"

"Done deal," he said.

"I like that," she agreed. "It's the right thing to do. But what about your brother and poor Penny? I mean—"

"Red, I know my brother. He may have started this thing with her for all the wrong reasons, but I finally calmed down enough to talk to him the other night and the guy's a mess right now. He says Penny won't have a thing to do with him, that he has no idea why. I didn't enlighten him. I'll leave that to your sister. But I think he's crazy about her."

Paige's mouth dropped open she was so shocked. "Really?"

Travis nodded. "Just convince her to come for Thanksgiving, and we'll see what happens."

"Did he actually tell you—"

"No, but just wait. I'm looking forward to watching him grovel."

"My brothers may kill him first," she warned.

"Okay, you're going to have to talk them out of that."

"You're right. Because Penny has a little surprise for your brother—"

"What?"

"Just wait. It's going to be a very interesting Thanksgiving. And that reminds me. I found something else in the mine while we were looking for the diamond, something I forgot to ask you about. A reddish crystal. I'd never seen anything like it before."

"A rock? You want to talk to me about a rock right now?"

"I like rocks," she reminded him. "These were really pretty. You know the ones I mean? Like a little bit of red fire trapped in crystal."

"Like you? Red fire?" He gave a soft, teasing kiss. "That's how I think of you. My own little red fire. My sweet red fire."

She laughed, gloriously happy. "This could really be something—"

"I think you're really something," he said, kissing her again.

And she knew, she wasn't going to have any kind of serious discussion with him about this right then.

But that red crystal…

How much could one woman possibly find on a ranch in Texas?

A man to love, a priceless treasure, and…

Well, maybe a brand-new gemstone.

Red fire.

For right now, she was content to be Travis Foley's red fire.

Another day, she'd figure out exactly what else she'd found on his ranch.

Epilogue

One month later

Travis walked in the door and felt like Christmas elves must have been at work in his house while he'd been out on the ranch.

There was a Christmas wreath with a big, red bow on the door, a tree inside beside the fireplace, decorated simply with little red ornaments and tiny, white twinkling lights, greenery spread across the mantle, red and white pillar candles everywhere.

Which could only mean, she was back.

Finally!

"Paige?" he called out.

He heard a little shriek from the direction of the

kitchen, and then she came running toward him, despite her high heels and fancy TV clothes. He caught her in his arms and kissed her like he'd never let her go.

"I didn't think you'd ever get back," he said.

She beamed up at him. "It was only four days."

"Felt like four dozen at least." And it had. It really had. Each time she'd gone, it had felt that way.

The house, the ranch, the entire world seemed empty now without her.

"Tell me you're done with all these press conferences and TV shows and all that," he demanded.

"I'm done! The whole world knows about the Santa Magdalena Diamond, and women everywhere want canary diamonds for themselves, just like Blake thought they would. I don't know how he did it, but he got the diamonds out to the stores this week, and they're selling like crazy. Just in time for Christmas."

"And how do you feel about a nice, quiet Christmas here at the ranch, just you and me?"

"I can't imagine anything better," she said, then made a face. "But I'm afraid—"

"No!" He knew what she was going to say. "Just us. Right here. No more—"

"Yes. We've been invited to a family get-together. Christmas Eve. Mom said everyone's coming."

Travis groaned. "They were just here for Thanksgiving. And it was nice. It was fine. We can do it again next year. How about that?"

"Oh, I think you're going to want to go," she claimed.

"No. I just want to be right here with you."

"But…I think there's something special for you there.

For Christmas. Since you've been so good this year," she said, looking at him in a way that had him thinking he was crazy to be standing here talking to her when he could have carried her off to bed already.

"I have everything I want already," he said, thinking of the engagement ring that had been delivered to the ranch while he was gone, custom made by her sister at his request, which he intended to put on her finger on Christmas Eve. If he had his way, they'd elope and she'd be his wife by New Year's

"No, you don't have everything yet," his red-haired beauty claimed. "There's one more thing. One big thing. A surprise. Just wait. You're going to love it."

* * * * *

*Celebrate 60 years of pure
reading pleasure with Harlequin®!
Just in time for the holidays,
Silhouette Special Edition®
is proud to present*
New York Times *bestselling author*
Kathleen Eagle's
ONE COWBOY, ONE CHRISTMAS

Rodeo rider Zach Beaudry was a travelin' man—
until he broke down in middle-of-nowhere South
Dakota during a deep freeze. That's when an angel
came to his rescue....

"Don't die on me. Come on, Zel. You know how much I love you, girl. You're all I've got. Don't do this to me here. Not *now*."

But Zelda had quit on him, and Zach Beaudry had no one to blame but himself. He'd taken his sweet time hitting the road, and then miscalculated a shortcut. For all he knew he was a hundred miles from gas. But even if they were sitting next to a pump, the ten dollars he had in his pocket wouldn't get him out of South Dakota, which was not where he wanted to be right now. Not even his beloved pickup truck, Zelda, could get him much of anywhere on fumes. He was sitting out in the cold in the middle of nowhere. And getting colder.

He shifted the pickup into Neutral and pulled hard

on the steering wheel, using the downhill slope to get her off the blacktop and into the roadside grass, where she shuddered to a standstill. He stroked the padded dash. "You'll be safe here."

But Zach would not. It was getting dark, and it was already too damn cold for his cowboy ass. Zach's battered body was a barometer, and he was feeling South Dakota, big time. He'd have given his right arm to be climbing into a hotel hot tub instead of a brutal blast of north wind. The right was his free arm anyway. Damn thing had lost altitude, touched some part of the bull and caused him a scoreless ride last time out.

It wasn't scoring him a ride this night, either. A carload of teenagers whizzed by, topping off the insult by laying on the horn as they passed him. It was at least twenty minutes before another vehicle came along. He stepped out and waved both arms this time, damn near getting himself killed. Whatever happened to *do unto others?* In places like this, decent people didn't leave each other stranded in the cold.

His face was feeling stiff, and he figured he'd better start walking before his toes went numb. He struck out for a distant yard light, the only sign of human habitation in sight. He couldn't tell how distant, but he knew he'd be hurting by the time he got there, and he was counting on some kindly old man to be answering the door. No shame among the lame.

It wasn't like Zach was fresh off the operating table—it had been a few months since his last round of repairs—but he hadn't given himself enough time.

He'd lopped a couple of weeks off the near end of the doc's estimated recovery time, rigged up a brace, done some heavy-duty taping and climbed onto another bull. Hung in there for five seconds—four seconds past feeling the pop in his hip and three seconds short of the buzzer.

He could still feel the pain shooting down his leg with every step. Only this time he had to pick the damn thing up, swing it forward and drop it down again on his own.

Pride be damned, he just hoped *somebody* would be answering the door at the end of the road. The light in the front window was a good sign.

The four steps to the covered porch might as well have been four hundred, and he was looking to climb them with a lead weight chained to his left leg. His eyes were just as screwed up as his hip. Big black spots danced around with tiny red flashers, and he couldn't tell what was real and what wasn't. He stumbled over some shrubbery, steadied himself on the porch railing and peered between vertical slats.

There in the front window stood a spruce tree with a silver star affixed to the top. Zach was pretty sure the red sparks were all in his head, but the white lights twinkling by the hundreds throughout the huge tree, those were real. He wasn't too sure about the woman hanging the shiny balls. Most of her hair was caught up on her head and fastened in a curly clump, but the light captured by the escaped bits crowned her with a golden halo. Her face was a soft shadow, her body a willowy silhouette beneath a long white gown. If this was where the mind ran off to when cold started shutting down the rest of the body, then Zach's final worldly thought was, *This ain't such a bad way to go.*

If she would just turn to the window, he could die looking into the eyes of a Christmas angel.

* * * * *

*Could this woman from Zach's past get
the lonesome cowboy to come in
from the cold...for good?
Look for
ONE COWBOY, ONE CHRISTMAS
by Kathleen Eagle
Available December 2009 from
Silhouette Special Edition*®

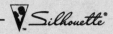

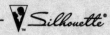

SPECIAL EDITION

FROM *NEW YORK TIMES* AND *USA TODAY*
BESTSELLING AUTHOR

KATHLEEN EAGLE

ONE COWBOY,
One Christmas

When bull rider Zach Beaudry appeared
out of thin air on Ann Drexler's ranch,
she thought she was seeing a ghost of
Christmas past. And though Zach had
no memory of their night of passion years
ago, they were about to share a future
he would never forget.

*Available December 2009
wherever books are sold.*

SSE65493

Visit Silhouette Books at www.eHarlequin.com

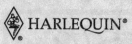

HARLEQUIN®

American ★ Romance®

A Cowboy Christmas
MARIN THOMAS

2 stories in 1!

The holidays are a rough time for widower
Logan Taylor and single dad Fletcher McFadden—
neither hunky cowboy has been lucky in love.
But Christmas is the season of miracles! Logan
meets his match in "A Christmas Baby," while
Fletcher gets a second chance at love in "Marry
Me, Cowboy." This year both cowboys are on
Santa's Nice list!

Available December
wherever books are sold.

"LOVE, HOME & HAPPINESS"

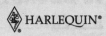

REQUEST YOUR FREE BOOKS!

2 FREE NOVELS PLUS 2 FREE GIFTS!

SPECIAL EDITION®

Life, Love and Family!

YES! Please send me 2 FREE Silhouette Special Edition® novels and my 2 FREE gifts (gifts are worth about $10). After receiving them, if I don't wish to receive any more books, I can return the shipping statement marked "cancel." If I don't cancel, I will receive 6 brand-new novels every month and be billed just $4.24 per book in the U.S. or $4.99 per book in Canada. That's a savings of at least 15% off the cover price! It's quite a bargain! Shipping and handling is just 50¢ per book.* I understand that accepting the 2 free books and gifts places me under no obligation to buy anything. I can always return a shipment and cancel at any time. Even if I never buy another book from Silhouette, the two free books and gifts are mine to keep forever.

235 SDN EYN4 335 SDN EYPG

Name	(PLEASE PRINT)	
Address		Apt. #
City	State/Prov.	Zip/Postal Code

Signature (if under 18, a parent or guardian must sign)

Mail to the Silhouette Reader Service:
IN U.S.A.: P.O. Box 1867, Buffalo, NY 14240-1867
IN CANADA: P.O. Box 609, Fort Erie, Ontario L2A 5X3

Not valid to current subscribers of Silhouette Special Edition books.

Want to try two free books from another line?
Call 1-800-873-8635 or visit www.morefreebooks.com.

* Terms and prices subject to change without notice. Prices do not include applicable taxes. Sales tax applicable in N.Y. Canadian residents will be charged applicable provincial taxes and GST. Offer not valid in Quebec. This offer is limited to one order per household. All orders subject to approval. Credit or debit balances in a customer's account(s) may be offset by any other outstanding balance owed by or to the customer. Please allow 4 to 6 weeks for delivery. Offer available while quantities last.

Your Privacy: Silhouette is committed to protecting your privacy. Our Privacy Policy is available online at www.eHarlequin.com or upon request from the Reader Service. From time to time we make our lists of customers available to reputable third parties who may have a product or service of interest to you. If you would prefer we not share your name and address, please check here. ☐

SSE09R

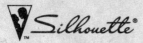
#2011 ONE COWBOY, ONE CHRISTMAS—Kathleen Eagle
When bull rider Zach Beaudry appeared out of thin air on
Ann Drexler's ranch, she thought she was seeing a ghost of
Christmas past. And though Zach had no memory of their night of
passion years ago, they were about to share a future he would never
forget.

#2012 CHRISTMAS AT BRAVO RIDGE—Christine Rimmer
Bravo Family Ties
Lovers turned best friends Matt Bravo and Corrine Lonnigan had
been there, done that with each other, and had a beautiful daughter.
But their affair was ancient history…until old flames reignited over
the holidays—and Corrine made Matt a proud daddy yet again!

#2013 A COLD CREEK HOLIDAY—RaeAnne Thayne
The Cowboys of Cold Creek
Christmas had always made designer Emery Kendall sad. But this
Cold Creek Christmas was different—she rediscovered her roots…
and found the gift of true love with rancher Nate Cavazos, whose
matchmaking nieces steered Emery and Nate to the mistletoe.

**#2014 A NANNY UNDER THE MISTLETOE—
Teresa Southwick**
The Nanny Network
Libby Bradford had nothing in common with playboy
Jess Donnelly—except for their love of the very special little girl
in Jess and Libby's care. But the more time Libby spent with her
billionaire boss, the more the mistletoe beckoned.…

#2015 A WEAVER HOLIDAY HOMECOMING—Allison Leigh
Men of the Double-C Ranch
Former agent Ryan Clay just wanted to forget his past. Then
Dr. Mallory Keegan came to town—with the child he never knew he
had. Soon, Ryan discovered the joy only a Christmas spent with the
little girl—and her beautiful Aunt Mallory—could bring.

**#2016 THE TEXAS TYCOON'S CHRISTMAS BABY—
Brenda Harlen**
The Foleys and the McCords
When Penny McCord found out her lover Jason Foley was using her
to get info about her family's jewelry-store empire, she was doubly
devastated—for Penny was pregnant. Would a Christmas miracle
reunite them…and reconcile their feuding families for good?